A Turning of the Tide

(Book 3: An Irish Family Saga)

Sequel to 'A Year of Broken Promises'

by

Jean Reinhardt

Historical Fiction

*'Even if the hopes you started out with are dashed,
hope has to be maintained.'*

<u>Seamus Heaney</u>

Dedication

To those who have emigrated from their native land, leaving family and friends behind.

Copyright

Title book: A Turning of the Tide

Author book: Jean Reinhardt

Text copyright © 2015 Jean Reinhardt

Cover illustration copyright © 2015 Jean
Reinhardt

Self-publishing

jeanreinhardt@yahoo.co.uk

CHAPTER ONE

Tom Gallagher surveyed the scene around him, making sure none of the other passengers were close by. The steamship carrying him and his younger brother across the Irish Sea was not as crowded as he had expected it to be. Their father warned them before they left home to keep to themselves and confide in no one.

"Am I going to die, Tom?" his brother whispered.

"Hush now, Patrick. If that were so, do you think Da would have let me take you away from him?"

Tom knelt down to where his brother sat on the wooden deck. As he unbuttoned the mid-section of Patrick's shirt, he saw that a patch of fresh blood had seeped through the cotton strips binding his narrow waist. Tom took a fresh wad of clean fabric from inside his jacket and looked around the deck once more. Noticing one of the crew coming in their direction, he quickly pulled his brother's jacket over the red stain.

"What ails your friend? Seasick, is he?" the man had stopped in front of them.

"Aye, he never was one for boats," replied Tom looking up. "He says he feels better lying down than walking around."

"Well, that may be so, but if he's about to lose his last meal the crew would prefer it was over the side, and not splattered across the deck. He's deathly pale."

"I'll be sure he makes it to the side and if he doesn't, I'll clean the mess up myself. Does that ease your mind?" Tom was getting annoyed.

The man gave a grunt and walked away, leaving the coast clear for a fresh wad of cotton to be placed on top of the open gash in the young man's side.

"Do I truly look that bad? I don't feel sick, Tom. Just weak."

"You've lost a lot of blood, Patrick, that's why you're so pale. If only that old codger knew what a good sailor you are, he wouldn't be at all worried about a mess on his deck."

"And if our clothes were made of finer fabric he would never have spoken to us in that manner," said Patrick.

"Be that as it may, but its talk like that has put you in this condition. You must learn to keep your opinions to yourself. Try to sleep now, before we dock. The longer you lie still the less blood you will lose."

As soon as Patrick closed his eyes he was asleep. Tom smiled, recalling his parents' laughter at how quickly their youngest child would nod off. A memory came back to him of a time in their home in Carlow, before circumstances forced them into the workhouse. Their mother had been late dishing up the supper and Patrick was rubbing his eyes, struggling to stay awake, in spite of his belly rumbling with the hunger.

Their father was chasing his daughters as they squealed around the cottage. Tom's mother had placed a platter of potatoes on the table and the two little girls ran towards the food. It was then they noticed Patrick asleep, his head resting on the rough wooden surface.

He remembered his father putting an arm around his mother's shoulders and both of them laughing at the snores of their youngest son. That was the only memory of his mother's face Tom allowed himself to carry – the one that blocked out the image of a fever ridden, starving woman.

When the ship docked, Tom helped his brother onto the quayside and left him sitting on the ground against a wall, while he sought out some transport.

Patrick took in the bustling scene around him. Try as he might, he could not remember the last time they had stood on the dockside in Dundalk, he had been far too young. Even his sisters' memories of Ireland were vague and his older brother refused to talk about it much. It was their father who had related the stories of his homeland to them, trying to keep alive the memory of their mother.

That was until he remarried, some years after they settled in England. Whenever Patrick or his sisters enquired about their mother the subject was changed, out of respect for his father's new wife. In time nobody asked and the memories began to fade.

As the scene around him turned hazy, Patrick heard his brother calling him. He felt strong arms lift him up from the ground and the blurred image of a donkey and cart appeared in front of him, before everything went black.

CHAPTER TWO

On seeing two strangers approach her cottage, Maggie leaned out to greet them and realized one was being supported by the other.

"Bless us and save us. Come in, come in," she fussed, opening the bottom of the half-door.

The day being sunny and fresh, the top part had been left open all morning to air out the cottage. Tom half carried his younger brother in through the doorway and looked around to see where he could sit him down.

"Over here, son. Lay him on that bed in the corner. He looks in a bad way, what ails him?" asked Maggie.

"He just needs to rest. Don't worry, it's not fever or anything like that. You are in no danger," said Tom.

"Thank goodness for that. Are ye looking for someone, or have ye just taken a long walk in the fresh air?" Maggie was used to visitors coming to Blackrock for the good of their health. "Are ye staying in one of the hotels in the village?" although she doubted that, by the state of their clothes.

Tom shook his head as he carefully helped Patrick down onto the settle bed. He felt nervous about telling a total stranger the true purpose of their visit.

"Do any of the McGrothers live here?" he asked. "We were told to ask for a Maggie McGrother at this house."

"I'm Maggie O'Neill by marriage, but everyone calls me McGrother on account of my brother, James. You just missed him by a day. He was here for a week with his wife, but they returned to England yesterday. In fact, I only came back to live in Blackrock, myself, not more than a month ago. James and Mary have returned to England to fetch their children. They should be back here in no time. Where have ye come from, son?"

"My father is Thomas Gallagher, do you recall him, Mrs. O'Neill? He is from Carlow but lives in Yorkshire now."

"Please call me Maggie. I can't say that I know your father. Did he live here in Blackrock at any time?"

"We lived in one of the fishermen's cottages for a few months with Pat and Annie McGrother. Their nephew James was in England at the time but his wife Mary was living with them and a young daughter by the name of Catherine. Am I correct in saying that, Mrs. McGro – Maggie?"

With an excited cry, Maggie threw her arms around the young man and hugged him tightly.

"It was *your* father, Thomas Gallagher, who painted the name on James's boat, wasn't it?" she asked.

Tom nodded, "I helped to repair the nets. Was your brother surprised to find he was the owner of a boat, on his return from England? I remember meeting him on the quayside just before we sailed to Liverpool."

"He was indeed, but that's another story. Let me put some water on the boil and you can tell me how your family is faring across the water."

While his brother dropped off to sleep, Tom chatted with Maggie about his sisters and his father and what type of employment they all had. Having slept for half an hour, young Patrick roused himself but cried out in pain as soon as he tried to sit up. Tom was at his side in an instant.

"Here you go, young man," Maggie handed Patrick a cup of hot tea and some bread.

"I'm much obliged to you ma'am, for the rest and the food. I hope I haven't inconvenienced you in any way."

"Well, there's manners for you. It's no trouble at all, son. Are you in a lot of pain?" Maggie turned to the older brother. "Do you think he needs a doctor, he's as white as my apron?" she looked down at her ash stained garment and quickly removed it.

Tom shook his head and asked if he could close the other half of the door, explaining that what he was about to divulge was for Maggie's ears alone.

"Of course you can. You're being very furtive, anyone would think ye had murdered someone."

The two young men exchanged nervous glances before Tom knelt beside his brother, opening his jacket wide. Maggie gasped at the sight of the blood stained shirt and ran to inspect what lay underneath. She shook her head at the sight that met her eyes. A gaping wound, three inches across and very deep, oozed fresh blood that threatened to drip down onto the blanket on which Patrick lay.

"I'll wash that out with some salted water and we can put a fresh dressing on it for you, but I think you need to see a doctor. That wound is very deep, I'm sure I can see some bone, most likely a rib."

"Please, Mrs. McGro. . . I mean, Maggie. Please don't tell a soul about this. Can you help him yourself? Isn't that what you want, Patrick?"

"I cannot go to a doctor. Will you explain the reason why, Tom?" Patrick had raised himself up on one elbow.

The older brother told Maggie that Patrick had been associating with a radical group, who were protesting against unsafe work conditions. One night, after a meeting in Sheffield, Patrick and some friends became involved in a disagreement with a group of men who had been following them. Tempers flared, knives were wielded and before anyone knew what had happened, a member of the rival gang lay dead and Patrick had a deep stab wound in his side.

"Someone helped my brother to get home and left him on our doorstep. Patrick refuses to say who it was or give us the names of the men he was with. This happened three nights ago. The police are investigating the death and my father is afraid that they may come looking for Patrick."

"Is there anything to connect you with that night, son?" asked Maggie.

Patrick shook his head, "It was only the second time I had attended one of their meetings. Sure I'm not even a member of the movement. Those men were sent to make trouble. I didn't recognize any of them and I'm sure they didn't know who I was either."

11

"Well then, let's be thankful for small mercies, shall we?" said Maggie. "I'm lodging in this house with another woman, Kitty Carroll. Her daughter wed last year and left for America with her husband, so there's only the two of us here now. She's down the road visiting a sick neighbour, but when she returns it will be up to her to decide what we should do with the two of ye. How long were you planning on staying in Ireland?"

"I will have to take the boat back to Liverpool tomorrow, but I would be much obliged if you could look after Patrick until he is well enough to fend for himself."

When Kitty arrived Maggie told her that Patrick was the son of an old family friend and in Blackrock for the good of his health. Kitty wouldn't hear of the young man fending for himself. She assured him that it would be good to have a man about the place, especially once Patrick had made a full recovery.

Early next morning, Tom bade farewell to his brother and the two women who had shown them such kindness. As he turned the corner at the top of the road, he looked back to see Patrick standing between Maggie and Kitty. Both women had an arm around the young man, who had insisted on going outside to say goodbye. They returned Tom's wave and as he picked up his pace towards Dundalk, he looked forward to being able to put his father's mind at ease with the news that his youngest son was in good hands.

CHAPTER THREE

Catherine sat by the stove and watched as the children played Blind Man's Buff. Thomas, who was blindfolded, stumbled around the kitchen table that stood in the centre of the parlour. He pretended to sniff out his younger siblings from their hiding places. Mary-Anne had opened the door and was ready to run into the street, while Brigid, whose nickname was Breege, and Jamie cowered under the table, clinging to each other in mock terror.

"I can smell where you are," Thomas said, reaching out his hands and walking towards Catherine. "When was the last time you bathed? What a stink."

His older sister pushed him away, laughing.

"You big fool, Thomas. Watch out for the stove."

The sound of muffled giggles came from underneath the table and Thomas quickly spun around, catching Breege as she tried to crawl out. After the usual penalty of a good tickling, Thomas let her go and handed the blindfold over.

"Go on outside now and continue the game with your friends," he said, dragging Jamie from his hiding place.

As they listened to the shouts and laughter coming from the street, the two older siblings sat on their parents' chairs, each side of the stove.

"They all love you, Thomas, even the neighbours' young ones, but they are afraid of me. I can see it in their faces," Catherine sighed.

13

"Do you think Mary-Anne is in fear of her own sister? Or Breege? What about Jamie? Sure he adores you. No, the children are just being respectful. It might help if you wore something a bit less fancy on your visits, though."

Catherine looked down at her dress, running her hands over the emerald green fabric. As a lady's maid she received all her mistress's hand-me-downs, to do with as she pleased. Her mother and aunts had been delighted to receive the dresses she passed on to them.

"You should have seen it when Mistress Eleanor wore it, full of bows and ribbons it was and fit to be called fancy. I have to remove all the decoration before I'm allowed wear it. Now it's just a plain old dress."

Thomas stoked up the fire and placed a large black kettle on the hotplate to boil.

"I had best not stay much longer. Jane will be expecting me back soon. I'm worried about leaving her alone for too long, she has been ill for most of the day."

"I still cannot believe that you are a married man and soon to be a father. I hope Jane doesn't have too hard a time, she's seems so young, compared to me that is. Are you happy with your life, Thomas?" asked Catherine.

"It would have been better for us if we had waited and had the time to save more money. But sure what's done is done and I love Jane dearly. It took two of us to make the baby, and it will take the two of us to raise it. Mr. Feeney has been very good to me and even increased my wages. As long as I can provide for us, I will be content enough with my life. And you, Catherine? Are you happy with yours?"

Catherine stood to make the tea as steam spouted from the kettle. She gave it a lot of thought before answering her brother's question.

"I'm satisfied with my lot, for now anyway. It would take a very special man to make me give it all up. I have my own room and I don't work half as hard as I used to. I am free to do as I please most Sundays. Sure at times, I even get to travel with the family. Did you know I was in Edinburgh not more than a month ago?"

"So I take it you won't be moving back to Ireland?" asked Thomas.

As she poured tea into two cups Catherine sighed deeply. She had expected her mother to be the one to insist on her leaving her job to return to Blackrock, but it had been her father who was most upset about her decision to remain in England.

"I told Ma and Da before they left for Liverpool that I had decided to keep my job. I said there would be no changing my mind. You should have seen the look on Da's face, anyone would think I had died."

"We always expect Ma to be the one that's more aggrieved. But in truth, it's Da we should worry about. He has a soft spot for his children, hasn't he? I hope I'll be the same with mine," said Thomas. "They should be back tomorrow evening. I pray the house that Maggie found for them is to Ma's liking or we'll never hear the end of it."

The conversation was interrupted by a loud cry from the street and then Mary-Anne's voice rang out, warning the other children to be careful.

"Mary-Anne has been quite the wee mother to the younger ones, hasn't she? Will your master give you leave to come home when they arrive?" Thomas asked.

"The family are having guests all week, so I may be expected to work next Sunday. I'm sure I can sneak away for a couple of hours one of the evenings, probably when everyone has gone to the theatre. There's a play on in Durham they have been planning on going to."

The children ran in from the street, Mary-Anne herding them to the table.

"I had better give these two a bite to eat before sending them up to bed," she said.

"Can we go with you, Thomas? Please," asked Breege. "Mary-Anne is such a bossy boots. She's worse than Ma."

"Sorry love, but not this evening. Jane is near her time and needs peace and quiet. Besides, your sister is doing a fine job taking care of you. Look how well fed you both are," Thomas pinched their cheeks.

"I'm nearly old enough to leave school," said Breege sullenly, "And I'm as tall as Mary-Anne. I don't need anyone to mind me."

Young Jamie was stuffing bread into his mouth faster than he could swallow it. Mary-Anne was a good cook and even better at baking than their mother.

"You could always get work on the docks," Jamie mumbled, his mouth full.

"What kind of work could I do there?" asked Breege.

"I don't know, but I heard Mrs. Cooney talking about Mrs. Halpin's daughter, the one that Ma says we are to stay away from and not even mention her name – that one. Mrs. Cooney said she earns a pretty penny on the docks and you look stronger than her, Breege. You would be sure to get lots of work there if she does."

Breege was horrified and stood up from the table, her face bright red.

"I'm pouring myself a cup of tea, does anyone else want one?" she asked.

Mary-Anne grabbed hold of Jamie, threatening to wash his mouth out with soap if he spoke like that again.

"What did I say? Thomas help me, don't leave me with her. I'll be murdered as soon as you're out the door and I don't even know what I've done."

Jamie had a terrified look on his face but he didn't fool his older brother, who was used to the young boy's dramatics.

"You'll survive. When you're a bit older I'll tell you what you said that got you murdered," Thomas smiled. "I had best be off now. I'll walk you back Catherine, it's not that far out of my way."

Having said their goodbyes, the two older siblings left the house, the sound of Jamie's squeals ringing in their ears.

"He sounds like a stuck pig, doesn't he?" laughed Thomas.

"Mary-Anne truly is a right little mammie. Ma would be lost without her," Catherine

17

linked her brother's arm and they walked in a comfortable silence for a long time.

"Can I ask you a question, Thomas? But I won't be offended if you prefer not to answer."

"Fair enough, what is it you want to know?"

"I've been reading a column in Mr. Feeney's paper these past few weeks. Someone by the name of R. E. Roubal writes it. Do you know him?"

"I've met him. Why do you ask, do you want an introduction?" laughed Thomas.

"Do I need one? Or am I looking at him now?"

Thomas wasn't surprised at his sister's observation. She had heard him on many occasions arguing with his parents over his radical views. He knew it was only a matter of time before someone in the family questioned him about the weekly column. Even his uncles, neither of whom could read, regularly bought the paper on account of their nephew's connection with it. Although their political views were far removed from Thomas's, they felt their support helped to keep him in a job.

"Keep it to yourself, Catherine. Even Mr. Feeney hasn't cottoned on. Not yet anyway."

"Be careful, Thomas, you have a wife and child to think of. Your heathen beliefs will get you into hot water, mark my words."

"I'm an atheist, Catherine, not a heathen. But don't dare tell Ma I said that. It would break her heart. Won't you get into trouble yourself, with your employers, if caught reading such a 'heathen' periodical?"

Catherine punched her brother in the arm and laughed. "I have to hide it in my underskirts to get it into the house. It burns very well in the fire, did you know that?"

"I'm not surprised, with all those fiery words by R. E. Roubal," replied Thomas.

"How did you come up with such an unusual name? Is it from one of your books?"

They stopped walking, having reached Catherine's destination. Thomas smiled as he said goodbye to his sister and backed away without answering her question.

"Thomas, I won't tell a soul. I promise."

"I believe you, Catherine. But I think I'll leave you figure it out for yourself," he shouted back as he turned and ran, his laughter echoing through the still air.

CHAPTER FOUR

"Are you sorry now that you didn't bring any of your own furniture with you?" asked James. "You will miss your stove, too, Mary."

"Not a bit. What's here will do us fine. Sure, look what's over there by the fire – a nice big pot and a kettle. Our mattresses and bedding are all that we needed to bring with us. And these, of course."

Mary pulled from a cloth bag the six wooden bowls she had inherited from James's aunt Annie. There was a good sized table against one of the walls and it was on this that Mary had placed the bags containing all of the family's possessions. The sound of laughter could be heard in the room overhead. James had sent the girls up with their mattresses.

"Those two are happy enough to be back, aren't they? And wee Jamie is still outside running around in the fresh air. I had better go and see what mischief he is getting up to in that overgrown plot we have behind us," said James.

Mary stepped in front of the doorway, blocking his exit.

"Before you go, tell me truthfully if you are happy enough yourself to be back in Blackrock. You've been so quiet this past week," she said.

James put his arms around his wife, assuring her that he was just having last minute doubts.

"You know the way I am, love. A worrier, even when things are going well. I fret over leaving Catherine behind and our Thomas with a young wife and baby to fend for."

"I do, too, James, but they are both old enough to care for themselves. Did we not raise them to be good people with common sense? But you are not alone with your worries, James. I myself become anxious at the thought of our first grandchild growing up so far away from us. Though she is not yet one month old I miss her sorely."

James admitted he felt the same way, "Thomas and myself agreed that we should try to meet up in Liverpool a year from now. I had not intended telling you as I wanted it to be a surprise. So, God willing, we shall see our wee Eliza next spring. Does that ease your mind, love?" asked James.

Mary was delighted with the news and seeing the look of joy on her face convinced James he had made the right decision in telling her of his plan.

"I'm off outside now to that bit of land we have at the back of the house to start digging," he said. "The sooner we get the ground ready for planting, the better. I'll get Jamie to help me, it will tire him out."

When Maggie arrived with a pot of stew Mary almost squeezed the life out of her, she hugged her so tight. They were all hungry but there wasn't much food left of what they had brought with them on the boat.

"Don't thank me too much, there's more bones than meat in that stew. Where's that brother of mine? I have someone I want ye to meet."

"He's out the back, digging. He brought his shovel over on the boat with him. Looked a proper navvy, he did," said Mary. "Who is it you want us to meet? Where are they?"

Maggie put her head back outside the door and called to someone. As she stepped inside, a slender young man with fair hair and the palest blue eyes Mary had ever seen, crossed over the threshold.

"Afternoon Mrs. McGrother," he said, removing his cap.

"Mary, this is Patrick, Thomas Gallagher's son, all the way from Yorkshire."

"Paddy-Patrick, or was it 'Not-Paddy-Patrick,' you were called by your family?" Mary smiled, shaking the hand held out to her.

"Nobody has called me that in years, I'm surprised you remembered."

"Have I been calling you by the wrong name then, son?" asked Maggie.

"My mother insisted that everyone call me by my full name. Whenever anyone shortened it to Paddy or Pat she would say, 'Not Paddy. Patrick,' and so that's what I said whenever I was asked what my name was. Even the neighbours began to call me Not-Paddy-Patrick, so it stuck."

"It's a bit of a mouthful, but if you like it so much, we can call you that," Maggie gave a sly smile.

Patrick assured the women that there was no need to do anything of the sort. He told them he had been relieved when his brother and sisters dropped the nick-name as he got older, only using it when they wanted to annoy him.

Mary called the girls downstairs, introducing them to their guest. She sent Breege outside to fetch her father and brother. As James welcomed the young man to his home, Mary dished up the stew into Annie's wooden bowls and Maggie broke up some bread to be dipped into it.

While the men talked, the children ate in silence, too busy devouring their meal. Mary-Anne was daintily taking small mouthfuls of bread and chewing it in an unusually lady-like fashion.

"What are you nibbling your bread like a wee mouse for, Mary-Anne? I hope you're not ailing," said Mary.

"There's nothing wrong with showing some manners at the table, is there? Not like those two savages there. You would think they hadn't eaten for a week," said Mary-Anne, her face colouring.

"Begging your pardon, m'lady. Do you want us to sit under the table where we can't offend you with our slurping and dribbling?" mocked Breege, who was sitting beside their guest.

Patrick was in conversation with James when he felt a sharp kick to his leg. Leaning to one side as he rubbed his shin, he frowned across the table at Mary-Anne.

"Was that boot meant for me?" asked Breege smugly.

Poor Mary-Anne's face went beetroot red as she excused herself to run upstairs. James decided it was time to leave the women to settle the children into their beds and asked Patrick if he would care to take a walk.

As soon as the men were gone Mary sent Breege upstairs to apologize to her sister. Jamie was tired from his work in the garden, and for once put up no resistance at being sent to bed.

"Did you see the way Mary-Anne was looking at Patrick? I thought she was going to swoon," said Maggie.

"Don't talk such nonsense, she's only a child," said Mary.

"She's fifteen. There are young ones married with a child at that age. I'm telling you, Mary, you had better have a word with her. She's a sensitive wee thing and I wouldn't like to see her getting hurt."

"By who? Patrick? Does that mean you plan on having a word with him, too?" asked Mary.

"I will if it comes to it, and no better woman to do it. You know I'm a straight talker. The next time Mary-Anne is in Patrick's company, take a keen interest in how she behaves and you'll see for yourself what I'm talking about. Will you do that much, at least?"

Mary nodded her head then changed the subject. She didn't want to think about either of her youngest daughters becoming women, especially not Mary-Anne.

CHAPTER FIVE

James received a warm welcome at Paddy Mac's from his old neighbours and fishing mates. They were already acquainted with Patrick and it was very obvious how well the young man fitted in.

"Well, you have certainly settled in here quickly enough," remarked James.

"Sure Patrick is one of our own now," said Paddy Mac. "How is your chest this evening, son?"

"Oh, it's not so bad today. I should be able to take up Joseph's offer of a place on his boat soon. That is, if it still stands?" said Patrick.

"What's wrong with your chest?" asked James.

"Pneumonia. That's why my father sent me here. I didn't have enough money for lodgings so Maggie and Kitty gave me bed and board in exchange for some work. Not that I can do much for now, my breathing being bad and all," Patrick forced a cough.

"That's a terrible sickness, I had it once myself," said James. "There's not much work you can do when that ails you. Put a hot whiskey in front of him, Paddy, that's what he needs."

Paddy Mac went through a door into the main house to put a drop of hot water into the whiskey. His premises had been licensed and extended, and in the summer, business was very good, with families visiting the village. They stayed in the various hotels and lodging houses of Blackrock that had sprung up over the years.

While the women liked the comfort of the hotel lounges, the men often came to Paddy Mac's for 'a real drink' as they called it. This made the locals smile, as the alcohol came from the same breweries and distilleries that delivered to the hotels. Everyone knew it was the atmosphere that attracted the visiting men.

"I put a bit of my wife's honey in that, son," said Paddy.

The young man looked at it, regretting having played along with Maggie's suggestion about the pneumonia.

"That's a woman's drink now, you're after ruining a good whiskey," Patrick was disgusted. "I thought fishermen drank rum anyway."

"Stop being an old woman and get it down you while it's still hot," laughed James, elbowing the young man in the ribs.

Patrick doubled over, instantly in pain, clutching his side. He had bitten into his lip to avoid yelling out.

"Here, sit down on this," James pulled over a low stool from a nearby table. "Either I'm a lot stronger than I thought or you're a very weak young fella," he said.

"I'll be fine . . . in a minute. I just got a sudden pain in my lung. Sure, you know yourself what that's like, James," said Patrick.

He had a hand inside his jacket pressing hard on the bandage that Maggie had changed earlier. James handed Patrick the whiskey, encouraging him to take small sips while it was still warm. Paddy Mac noticed beads of sweat forming on the young man's forehead and handed him a cloth.

"Here, son. Take this and mop your brow, you might be running a fever."

Patrick automatically took his hand out from beneath his jacket to reach for the cloth and James was taken aback to see that his fingers were blood-stained. He glanced at Paddy Mac, who nodded and gestured toward the store room at the back of the premises. James put an arm around Patrick and hoisted him up, steering him towards a door held open by Paddy Mac.

"I don't know what's wrong with young men these days, can't hold their liquor, can they?" chided James as they passed by two men standing at the bar.

"Ah, go easy on him. He's been used to that watered down ale they serve up, over yonder," laughed one of the men.

"Aye, you might not be far wrong there," said James.

Sitting on a barrel, with Paddy Mac down on one knee examining the wound in his side, Patrick felt guilty for misleading the two men. Nobody said a word for a few minutes then James cleared his throat.

"So, pneumonia is it? And who exactly diagnosed your ailment. Would it have been my sister by any chance?"

Patrick clenched his teeth as Paddy Mac poured a little alcohol into the freshly opened gash. The young man's side felt as if it were on fire and tears stung at his eyes with the pain.

The little store room at Paddy Mac's had often been used as a place to bind up cuts and gashes, including the odd gunshot wound. He could tell it was a knife that had made the incision but waited for Patrick to own up to James about it himself.

"Well? Are you going to enlighten us as to how you came about that hole in your side, or do I have to question Maggie?" James's patience was wearing thin.

Patrick sighed, then told them about the incident in England and why his father had sent him away.

"I'll leave in the morning. I don't want to bring any trouble to your doors."

"Don't be so hasty, son. There's been no word here of that particular incident. Sure it's not like it took place in Liverpool, Sheffield is far enough away," said James. "If Maggie and Kitty are happy to have you stay, who am I to say any different? Do you think either of those two women would listen to me anyway?"

The three men laughed and Patrick fastened his jacket as he stood up. Paddy Mac assured him that his secret was safe with him.

"If these walls could speak of the things said and done in this room, I'd have been hung, drawn and quartered long ago."

CHAPTER SIX

There was something different about the room James sat in. The walls appeared to be unchanged and the furniture seemed to be in the same position as before. In fact, James felt as if it was only a short time ago he had been in that same office, handing over a bag of money to the man opposite him.

"I cannot believe it's been a decade since you last sat at my desk, James."

At the mention of the piece of furniture, it dawned on James what was different about his surroundings.

"I'm not sure I ever sat at this desk, Mr. Harrington. Is it new?"

"How very observant of you. Yes it is. My wife surprised me with it a year ago, my clerk also received one – although he is a lot more enamoured with his desk than I am with mine. I much preferred the old one. But of course I would never admit that to my wife, she still runs her fingers lovingly along the wood every time she comes here."

"Your man outside should be thankful you don't change clerks as often as your wife changes the furniture," said James and both men laughed. "I want to thank you, Mr. Harrington, for not handing over my money to Lord Devereux. His death would have put an end to any hope of having it returned."

"I'm happy that you don't bear me any resentment for going against your wishes at the time, James. I knew the Freemont estate was in some financial difficulty, but I was not at liberty to tell you. Even with your uncle exonerated, your money would have been absorbed to offset some of the debt."

"Well I'm much obliged to you for that, and for this," James held a piece of paper containing his signature in the air. "I have been teasing Mary about a gift I plan on giving her, she will think this is it."

"A year's rent paid in advance is indeed a wonderful gift. I daresay she will be delighted."

"Ah, but there is one more gift to come, and I cannot wait to see her face when it arrives," said James.

Just as he was about to inquire what the surprise for Mary might be, two sharp knocks sounded on the door. The solicitor's clerk entered the room, frowning.

"I'm very sorry to disturb you, sir, but a telegram has arrived with regard to a situation in Dublin."

"Oh, I was hoping that would be avoided. I'm sorry, James, I must attend to this matter straight away. If you need anything at any time, please do let me know," William Harrington stood, holding out a hand to his client.

James grasped it firmly and knew that the words spoken were genuine.

"I must be away, myself, I have an ass and cart to buy. That's my surprise for Mary. Good day to you Mr. Harrington."

The children clapped their hands with joy to see their father arriving with their new mode of transport. James sat the three of them on the cart and inquired about their mother's whereabouts.

"She's at the back of the house, planting the cuttings that Mrs. Carroll gave her. I'll fetch her for you, Da," Breege jumped down.

"Don't tell her about the ass and cart. We'll surprise her," said James.

Mary stumbled around the corner of the house, with Breege alongside, covering her mother's eyes with her hands.

"If I trip and break my neck, you'll pay dearly my girl."

"You can stop walking now, Ma," said Breege, taking her hands away. "Open your eyes."

Mary gasped and stood beside her husband to stroke the animal's head. James lifted her up onto the cart and handed her the reins.

"Here, take the children up to the end of the road and back, love. Then we'll let Breege and Jamie settle him in his new home," he said.

"So this is why you made the outhouse bigger. I thought Matthew Clarke had come to live with us, he was here so often with his cart full of stones for you," laughed Mary.

Maggie called later that evening and was introduced to the donkey by the children.

"He's a fine animal, what are ye going to call him?" she asked.

"I want to call him Thomas," piped up Jamie.

"After your brother?" asked Maggie.

The young boy nodded his head, "But Da says we have to give him an Irish name. I thought Thomas *was* Irish, he was born here wasn't he?"

James smiled at his son's innocence and picked him up, swinging him effortlessly over his shoulder, "You're just an old sack of turnips. Only fit for the pig sty, Jamie," he said.

"Why don't ye call him Rí, that's the Irish for king? Sure doesn't he look like he's the king of the asses?" suggested Maggie.

The children agreed that it was a fine name and made up a song about it as they led him to the back of the house.

"I have a sack of seed potatoes on the cart, Mary, we can plant them tomorrow and we'll have our own crop to eat by July."

"I can bring young Patrick over with me and we'll give you some help. His lungs have been clearing up nicely, breathing in the fresh sea air these past few months," said Maggie.

James rolled his eyes, unseen by either women, as he lifted the sack from the cart. Patrick's secret had remained safe and Maggie was still unaware of what had taken place in Paddy Mac's storeroom.

"We would be much obliged for the help, Maggie. Wouldn't we James?"

"Aye, we would at that, Mary. I'll just bring these round to the outhouse and rescue that poor old *king* from his subjects."

A week later, James and Mary stood surveying their small patch of land. They had planted cabbage, onions, parsnips, potatoes and two apple trees. A fence made up of intertwining branches separated the vegetables from where a brood of hens pecked about on some upturned sods.

"I cannot believe we have only been back home less than a fortnight," Mary said.

"Everything is more or less done now, so I'll be going out on Matthew Clarke's boat tonight. Not for an equal share of the catch, though. He has a full crew, but when I told him how much I had missed being out in the bay, he said I could join them anytime. No doubt I'll bring back some fish for the family."

"Do you wish you had your own boat again, James?" asked Mary.

"I would be lying if I were to say I don't. But when I see what we've done here and the relief on your face with no rent to worry about for twelve months, then I don't think I would want to exchange that for any boat, no matter how grand it was," said James.

"Speaking of rent, what did Mr. Harrington have to say about you repairing the walls and outhouses of the gentry? Does he think they will still be wary of a McGrother around their property? We will soon have to start thinking about next year's rent."

"And everyone thinks it's me that is the worrier in the family. That's a long way off, Mary, don't be fretting over debts we don't even have yet. William say's that people have short memories and with Armstrong off my back and stationed far enough away, there is no reason why I cannot canvass for work at the big houses."

Mary laughed and gave a small courtesy.

"So, its William now, is it? I beg your pardon, m'lord, I would have dressed better had I known of your visit."

"I'll forgive you this time, m'lady," James gave a mock bow. "Mr. Harrington said I should call him William, but I have never been able to do so – at least not to his face."

Mary lowered her voice to a whisper and James bent his head to hear what she was saying.

"What was that you said about Mr. Harrington? I can barely hear you," said James.

."Maggie told me that there's talk he is a sympathizer to the cause," whispered Mary.

James grabbed her by the arm and led her towards the house. Having made sure that the children were not within earshot, he whispered a reply.

"Maggie should not be discussing politics with you. She can do as she pleases but you cannot. Are you listening to what I'm saying?" James shook his wife's arm.

Mary, who had been anxiously looking around them as he spoke, turned her face towards James and glared at him.

"Do not treat me like an imbecile, and release my arm this minute, James McGrother. Or do you want the neighbours to think that you beat your wife?"

James loosened his grip on Mary's arm and she wrenched it free, rubbing where his fingers had pinched her flesh.

"What I said was only heard by yourself and that inoffensive animal yonder," Mary pointed towards the donkey. "In future I will make sure that you are not within earshot when I'm speaking to the ass."

"I'm sorry, love, but there are some who believe that printing periodicals and openly admitting to being sympathetic to the Fenians will help the movement gain support. Others are more wary and prefer to remain discreet, not drawing attention from the government in Dublin. I am of the latter opinion," said James.

"You mean secretive. Well I am not of the latter. I'm tired of having to pay heed to what I say, where I say it, and who I say it to. Can a person not form an opinion, James? Your sister has done so."

"Maggie only has herself to worry about. We have children and a grandchild to keep in mind. You can form as many opinions as you like, Mary, but keep them to yourself. Do you not think I have my own thoughts and feelings on Irish politics?" James glanced around him before continuing. "Of course I have, but I do not share them with anyone, and I'm not asking you to be more discreet, Mary – I'm *telling* you. Armstrong may be in another county, but I can assure you, he has not forgotten our family. Mr. Harrington informed me that the man is now a district inspector, with even more power than he had before. It's only a matter of time before he turns his attention once more in my direction."

"Fine, James. I understand what you are telling me and I promise to be more careful from now on. However, it's not me you need to counsel, but your sister – and we both know that Maggie would nod her head at your words, then do as she pleases anyway."

CHAPTER SEVEN

Henry Armstrong peered through a tiny hatch, inhaling deeply as he did so. His father had been a carpenter and the faint scent of oak from the cell door reminded the inspector of the smell of wood from his father's clothes. It had been his ritual to lift his young son high upon his shoulders, as soon as he arrived home from his day's work, tired but always smiling. It was Henry's favourite childhood memory.

The prisoner, tied to a chair in the centre of the small rectangular cell, was unaware of his audience. Henry Armstrong could see the determination set in the battered face. With such bruised and swollen features, it would have been difficult for even the young man's mother to identify him, never mind a witness.

The inspector turned to the constable at his side and gestured for him to move further along the corridor.

"How many times do I have to tell you not to cause any disfigurement to the face? There are plenty of less obvious areas on the body that are a lot more sensitive and unlikely to be seen. How can we pay a witness to identify him now? It will take far too long for the swelling to go down. You had better pray that William Harrington is not called upon to represent him."

"Sorry, sir. He spit in my face one time too many. It won't happen again," the young constable avoided eye contact with his superior officer as he answered.

"Did you manage to get any useful information out of him?"

The response was a shake of the head.

"I thought as much. If it wasn't for the informers that have infiltrated their so-called Brotherhood we would have nothing to act upon," said Armstrong. "Untie him and make sure you aim for a more discreet place next time he decides to share his spittle with you. I've been summoned to Dublin and will probably be there overnight. Try not to kill him before I get back."

Francis Kiernan could barely see through his swollen eyelids. The one thing that had kept him from breaking, during his ordeal at the hands of an out of control constable, had been the image of his mother's face. The last time he saw her was when she kissed him goodbye on the pier in New York, just before he boarded the ship to England. Francis had seen the tears in her eyes, in spite of the smile she wore.

As long as he admitted to nothing he knew the chances were good he would be sent back to America. That's what his father and other members of the Brotherhood had always told him. Besides, he had his American papers and he had done nothing wrong, except attend a couple of meetings and organize a fund raising.

Francis's mother, Brigid, had no idea of her son's involvement with the organization that his father so passionately supported. She was under the impression that her eldest son was on a visit to Liverpool, to stay with her sister and his cousins. When he broached the subject of a trip to Dundalk to call on what few relatives remained there, his mother made him swear that he would not step foot on Irish soil. She was afraid that he might attract the attention of the militia because of his father's reputation.

At the sound of keys rattling in the corridor, Francis, although weak and exhausted, automatically stiffened his body, preparing for another blow. The young constable who entered his cell, gave him a sympathetic smile and untied his hands. Having led Francis from the chair to a bed, he placed a bucket of cold water and some rags beside the young prisoner, so he could tend to his wounds. Not a word was exchanged between them as the constable left the cell.

The coolness of the water was soothing to his swollen face, but stung the open cuts and grazes, making Francis wince at each touch of the wet cloth. Finding himself alone for the first time since his arrest the day before, the young man slowly relaxed the muscles in his body, allowing a much needed sleep overtake him.

CHAPTER EIGHT

Catherine could not believe how much she was missing her family. Barely a month had gone by since her parents and younger siblings had returned to Ireland, yet it felt more like a year.

"Sure you have me and Jane and little Eliza. Is that not comfort enough for you?" asked Thomas.

Looking down at the tiny bundle cradled in her arms, Catherine felt a warm glow in the pit of her stomach.

"I wish it could be, but I think I am missing more than just the family. I envy you and Jane, Thomas. I know you both struggle, making ends meet, but you have each other. As long as I remain in the doctor's house there will be little chance of me finding a husband. If I do, I will no longer have employment as a lady's maid."

Thomas wasn't sure how to respond. In truth, it saddened him to know that his sister should feel lonely, and he felt guilty for not spending more time with her.

"Not everyone is suited to marriage, Catherine. Maybe you should not think about it until you meet someone that is worth giving up your position for."

"Now that's an easy thing for a man to say. It's different for a woman, after a certain age there is less chance of finding a husband. Men in their fifties can find a wife if they care to. If I let too many years go by, I might as well become a nun. Do you think that would make Ma happy?" asked Catherine, handing the baby to her brother. "I had best be getting back. Don't disturb Jane, let her sleep, and take good care of this wee beauty until I see ye again."

Thomas smiled at the thought of his older sister joining a convent. If Mary-Anne had made that statement it wouldn't have surprised him at all, but Catherine would never suit the life of a nun. She would be thrown out of the convent within a month, for causing a riot.

As soon as the door closed, Thomas heard a creaking overhead and knew that his wife would appear at the bottom of the stairs within minutes. He lay the baby in her cradle, and positioned the kettle on the stove top to boil the water.

"Has Catherine left already? I was hoping to say goodbye."

"You know full well she has gone, Jane. She really doesn't mind if you stay with us until she leaves. I don't either, there's no need to feign tiredness to give us time alone," said Thomas.

"I really was tired. Besides, you do the same when my sisters are here. Or is that because you have an aversion for their silly prattle?"

Thomas turned to look at his wife's face and saw her smiling. It was true that he loathed their idle gossip and conversations about such mundane things as bonnets and shoes.

"That's because they never speak of anything important, Jane. I can hear them breathe a sigh of relief as soon as I walk out the door."

"What you would class as silly things are important to them, Thomas. They're still young, it will all change as soon as they become old married women, like their sister."

"You were never that flippant. It's what drew me to you," Thomas noticed a change in Jane's face. "Are you feeling ill? You look as pale as your nightgown."

"Just the old complaint, love. I won't get any better, I'm likely to get worse. You'll be sorry you took me on, Thomas," Jane smiled sadly.

Her husband picked her up and carried her towards the stairs, "Then you had best sleep some more my love, I shall keep watch on Eliza."

As Jane settled herself into the still warm bed, she grasped Thomas's hand, "Promise that if anything should happen to me, you will take Eliza to your parents. It will be impossible for you to manage her on your own and my Ma has her hands full as it is. Besides, I don't want my daughter to go through the same nightmare I did with Da and his drinking. Promise me now, or I won't be able to sleep."

"Are you feeling worse, Jane? Is that what's brought this on? How many times have I refused to swear that oath to you, my love," the young man stroked the fair wavy hair that lay strewn across the pillow. "I have never for one second regretted being wed to you. If I have to take on more work to keep up your treatments so be it. Now, I want *you* to make *me* a promise. Swear to me that you will get better."

Jane turned her head towards the window and saw that it was getting dark outside. She wished that, like her husband, her faith meant nothing to her and that she could grant him his wish. Lying was not a thing that came easily to either of them.

"What are we like?" she smiled, cupping her husband's face in between her palms. "Neither of us willing to say the words the other wants to hear. Go on back downstairs now and let me steal some more sleep, before Eliza wakes up again."

Thomas leaned over to kiss her pale, clammy forehead, then stepped out of the room without uttering a word. He knew in his heart that Jane would never leave her mother so there was no point in repeating his request that they pack up and join his parents in Ireland.

Thomas stood, leaning against the doorframe, watching as his young wife drifted into a restless sleep. After a very long time, he turned and left the room. As he reached the bottom of the stairs, the door opened and a cold draught followed two young men into the house. They were lodgers, working in the same mill that had caused Jane's health problems."

"There's a wee bit of broth left if you'd like some."

"Thank you, Thomas. It's just what we need on a chilly night like this. How is Jane faring this evening?" asked one of the men.

"Not so good, I'm worried that she is getting worse, especially since Eliza was born. My Aunt Rose gives us medicine she gets from the hospital but it hasn't improved her much."

The two men gave each other knowing glances while drinking their broth, but said nothing.

"Do ye not hold out much hope for Eliza's recovery? I would prefer that ye were truthful with me," Thomas sat at the table with them. "I have been trying to prepare myself for the worst these past few weeks."

"Have any of your family ever worked in the mills?" asked one of the lodgers.

Thomas shook his head, "All the men and boys either work in the foundries or quarries and my female cousins are mostly domestics, as was my sister at one time."

"We've seen Jane's symptoms before. Especially on those who have worked in the mills since childhood, breathing in the dust and fibres. The new vents help but they've come too late for the likes of Jane," said the older of the two. "I know she's barely nineteen, Thomas, but she has the lungs of an old woman. Sooner or later the heart gives out from the strain. Some of us are affected more than others. My own mother died in her twenties. It was my grandmother who reared me."

Their conversation was interrupted by a loud cry and Thomas quickly lifted his baby daughter from her crib.

"Hush now, my wee angel, and let your mother have a few more minutes of sleep," he soothed.

There was no comforting the hungry infant and Thomas excused himself. By the time he reached the top of the stairs, Jane had opened the bedroom door to him, a heavy shawl draped across her shoulders.

"Don't look at me with such a scowl on your face. I cannot remain in bed all day. I need to look at something other than these four walls," Jane took the fretful baby from her husband's arms. "See how she quietens at the sound of my voice. Why can't you do that?"

They both laughed as Thomas turned to lead the way back down the stairs.

The lodgers greeted Jane then quickly excused themselves, to head up to the second bedroom they shared. Their workday began at five o'clock each morning and it would take a special occasion to keep them up past ten at night.

"Don't go on my account, men. I'm sure the three of you were having a grand old natter before her ladyship here made her presence known," said Jane.

Assuring her that it was close to their bedtime the men left the parlour, giving the young family their privacy.

While Thomas made some tea he could hear his daughter grunting as she nuzzled into her mother's breast, in search of sustenance. It crossed his mind to try once more to talk Jane into moving to Ireland with him, but when he turned and saw the peaceful, contented look upon his wife's face, he changed his mind. He would wait until another day to bring up a subject they could never agree on.

CHAPTER NINE

Michael Kiernan paced back and forth across the dirt floor in the outhouse, where he had been sleeping for almost a week. The message he had received caused him to feel elated yet anxious at the same time. It was not that the news was anything different from what had been relayed to him on numerous occasions, but this time it was about his own son.

The mellow voice of a man sitting on an upturned crate broke through his racing thoughts and Michael stopped in his tracks.

"Can you please repeat those words, I hope I have not misheard you."

"Your son will be with you in a matter of hours. Two of my men happened to be incarcerated in the same jail as your young man and we were able to get all three of them out this evening."

"But he has American papers, surely they could not have detained him for much longer," said Michael.

"His papers would not have ensured his release. I'm afraid the crown does not recognize a change to American citizenship when it comes to one of its own subjects. With the suspension of *habeas corpus* he could have been held indefinitely," the mellow voice replied. "I must warn you, from what I have been told, your son's treatment has not been the best at the hands of the inspector. One of the constables is a sympathizer and it was he who informed us of Armstrong's trip to Dublin. An armed escort accompanied him leaving fewer men to guard the prisoners. It was the perfect opportunity to get our men out."

"Armstrong, I know that name. Was he at one time stationed in Dundalk?" asked Michael.

"He was indeed, and everyone there breathed more easily once he was moved elsewhere. He's a dangerous man, not because he meticulously carries out his duties to the crown, but for a more unsettling reason – he loathes the Irish. Hatred has a way of driving common sense out of a person. Armstrong makes his decisions based on his emotions and that will be his downfall, mark my words."

"I have never met this man, but some years ago a good friend of mine was a victim of Armstrong's persecution. His poor old uncle died while in his custody, for something he was blameless of," said Michael.

"Would your friend's name be McGrother, by any chance?"

Michael felt his heart skip a beat, "How could you know that? Is James a member of the Brotherhood now?"

The man with the mellow voice stood to stretch his legs.

"Not that I am aware of. Let's just say I was privy to information concerning his situation. You say he is a good friend, does that mean you know him well enough to trust him with your life?"

Michael considered the question for a few moments. It was a difficult one to answer as there had been little correspondence between himself and James.

"If it takes you this long to reply, then be careful not to put your friend in a position where he might have to prove his loyalty to you."

"James's family comes before anything else. He loves Ireland because this is where his heart is but his love for his wife and children will always have first place," said Michael.

"And what about yourself? Surely you love your family just as much."

"My heart is with my family, but I left them long ago. I chose Ireland over them. My country is not in my heart, she's in my blood. That's the difference between James and myself. He lives for the present and hopes for a better future. I live only for the future. Is that not the same for you, Robert?" asked Michael.

There was a few seconds of silence and then a quiet chuckle.

"So, you know who I am. Yes, it is the same for me. We are cut from the same cloth, you and I. That is why we are in a position of leadership. Not everyone is suited to it, Michael," Robert sighed and shrugged his shoulders. "I must leave you now, my friend. A doctor is on his way, your son will have need of him. Have no fear, he will be discreet and you can trust him implicitly."

The two men shook hands. "Remember this conversation, when you next lay eyes on your boy. Try not to let your anger get the better of you, Michael. You hold the lives of your comrades in your hands, so for their sakes, do not be tempted to make rash decisions."

When he was once again alone, someone brought Michael a supper of tea and bread but the begging eyes of the dog that had been keeping him warm each night got the better of him. As he watched the animal rummage in the dry earthen floor for every last crumb, Michael was reminded of the years of hunger, sickness and famine he had lived through as a young man.

Even in a village with the sea on its doorstep and landlords that were not as harsh as in some of the other counties, starvation had been an ever present danger and with it came disease. Michael was thankful that his own children had never experienced such hunger that drove a person to eat grass, until they died with their lips stained green.

******

Across the Irish Sea a young man was deep in conversation with his aunt and uncle about a decision no one should have to face at such a tender age.

"I'm sorry, love, but Jane has accepted her fate and you must, too," said Rose.

"I cannot. I will not. Even if I must force her to come with me, she is far too weak to put up any resistance. She will thank me for it when her health improves."

"Thomas, you know full well that two different doctors at the hospital have examined Jane and neither of them gave ye any hope. Do you think your wife will thank you for letting her die with none of her family by her side?" asked Rose. "Her mother and sisters were all she had before you came along, son. Would you deny them these last few months together?"

"Rose, go easy on the lad. There's nothing wrong with being hopeful," said Owen.

"Aye, maybe you're right," Rose stood over her grief stricken nephew and cupped his chin in her hand. "Trust your heart, Thomas, and you'll make the right decision. I'm off to tackle the laundry and leave the pair of ye alone to talk man to man."

CHAPTER TEN

"Molly Sinnott told me that if you kiss a boy with your mouth closed you won't get pregnant," whispered Breege, "I thought you had to do a bit more than open your mouth. I asked Ma and she said she would tell me when I was older. Then she made me scrub the bedroom floors for hanging about with the Sinnotts."

Mary-Anne turned on her side to face her sister and spoke in a hushed voice. Neither of them wanted their younger brother to hear the conversation they were having, and the snores coming from the opposite side of the room indicated that he was fast asleep.

"Don't mind what she says. She told me her cousin got pregnant first time she 'did it' with a fella and she wasn't even fond of him."

"No wonder Ma forbid us go near that family. What do you mean by she 'did it'? What exactly did she do?" asked Breege.

"I'm not really sure," lied Mary-Anne, "But whatever it was, the fella told her he would have to do it again to finish making the baby. He said it would have no arms or legs if he didn't."

"Merciful heaven, and she didn't even like him," gasped Breege. "Could she not have 'done it' with someone else that she was fond of?"

"Molly's cousin asked the very same question, and the fella told her that it had to be the same man or the limbs wouldn't stick," Mary-Anne glanced over to where Jamie was lying and listened to his breathing before

50

carrying on. "He told her that some babies were even born with no heads because the woman wouldn't allow the man to finish making it."

Breege's hands flew to her mouth to smother a gasp of horror. The image of headless babies would give her nightmares for sure but she didn't want to finish the conversation.

"I've never seen a baby with no head. I saw one with half an arm, though."

"Sure if they have no head they can't breathe or eat. That's why we don't see them crawling about, Breege. Have a bit of sense, girl."

The sisters covered their mouths with their hands to contain their laughter, until Jamie coughed and turned over, temporarily silencing the two of them.

"Is that why you have to get married and stay with the same man? To make sure the child has all its bits and pieces – and a head," whispered Breege.

"No. You have to get married because it's a sin to 'do it' if you're not. But maybe that's why God made it a sin, to stop poor unfortunate babies being born with parts missing. Now turn around and let me get my sleep, and don't you dare repeat a word of what I told you to Ma, or she'll have the both of us strung up. Do you hear, Breege?"

Having assured her sister that their mother would be none the wiser about their conversation that night, Breege turned her back to Mary-Anne and closed her eyes. Counting backwards from a hundred, she tried to dismiss the images of partially formed babies from her head, before falling asleep.

Downstairs, James and Mary lay in each other's arms, listening to the familiar crash of waves on the shore not too far from their house. Neither of them could sleep, having received a letter that day from their eldest daughter. The sound of muffled laughter coming from above brought a smile to James's face.

"Those two are pulling each other's hair out one minute, then falling about laughing the next," he said.

"That's what sister's do," replied Mary. "Speaking of sisters, I cannot get Catherine's words out of my mind, James. Poor Thomas, do you think I should go over?"

"I was lying here thinking about that letter myself, Mary. If Thomas wanted either of us to be with him, he would ask. Owen and Rose are there for him, he was always close to them. There's nothing we can do for now, love. He'll need us when the time comes for Jane to go."

James kissed Mary's forehead and offered up a quick prayer of gratitude that he still had her by his side, in spite of the hard times they had lived through. He couldn't bear to think about the pain his son was going through at that moment.

Something else began to play on James's mind and he knew it would be unwise of him to share it with his wife, or his sister, Maggie. Matthew Clarke had forwarded a message from Michael Kiernan that greatly disturbed James.

His son, Francis, had been on his way to visit his father's uncle in Blackrock but was taken into police custody, as soon as he stepped off the boat from Liverpool and onto the pier in Dundalk. Michael himself was in hiding, having being involved in various incidents against the militia.

James was only slightly surprised that his friend was not in America, as he had led everyone to believe. He had a feeling that Francis Kiernan's trip to Ireland was for more than just a friendly visit to a relative. He gently pulled his sleeping wife closer to him and she placed her arm across his chest. There was a special bond between them that could never be broken, not even in death. James knew that Mary felt the same way and neither of them would hesitate to lay down their life for the other.

A sudden feeling of panic caused his heart to pound in his chest and James eased Mary's arm away, for fear she, too, may feel it. As anxious thoughts raced through his head, a sense of imminent danger swept over him. James tried to put it down to the approaching death of his son's ailing wife, but deep in his heart he knew that grief of a different nature was about to pay him a visit.

CHAPTER ELEVEN

The sight of Mary-Anne standing on the shore waving at them brought a smile to James's face. Of late, if the air was not too chilled, his daughter had been allowed to replace his wife in bringing the fish to market on one of the carts. It was a good feeling for a man to arrive back from a night out in the bay and have a woman welcoming his safe return.

Although a love of the sea was in itself as good a reason as any to be a fisherman, providing for a family made it even more rewarding. James had never once taken for granted the sight of Mary standing on the rocks, waiting for him. He felt blessed that even in inclement weather, when the sea was too rough to bring a boat out, he could always find a wall to mend or an outhouse to build. The same storms that prevented him from being out in the bay often tore down trees and left damaged walls and buildings, thus providing some work to make up for the lack of fishing.

James and Mary had given in to the begging and pleading of their second eldest girl, Mary-Anne. They had agreed that as long as the fine weather lasted, she could go to market in her mother's place, with her father's share of the catch. Mary was happy to spend the extra time tending to her vegetables. She had lived in a town long enough to have lost interest in the buzz of urban life, whereas, Mary-Anne loved it.

Mary was not ignorant of the fact that the teenage girl had her sights set on young

Patrick Gallagher, which accounted for her sudden interest in meeting the boats coming ashore. As a mother, she hoped her daughter would find a suitable husband but she was not sure that Mary-Anne had what it took to be a fisherman's wife. It was a hard life and when children came along it became even more difficult.

Patrick was aware of his admirer's affections and had been careful not to lead such a young girl on. He considered her still a child and felt sure that her parents had noticed how she behaved in his company. Neither of them had mentioned it to him, if they had.

"Isn't it high time you got yourself a wife, Patrick," said James in a serious tone of voice.

The young man felt as if his thoughts had been read. He glanced behind as he rowed, to see if James was smiling, but his companion wore a serious expression on his face as he looked out into the bay.

"I haven't met the right one yet, James. Besides, what do I have to offer? No land, no regular work and no savings. Would you consider me a good prospect for one of your daughters?"

"If young Lord Deveroux himself asked for any of my girls' hands I would have a mind to refuse him. Do you know why, Patrick?" asked James.

"No, I don't?"

The other fishermen had begun to take an interest in the conversation.

"Tell him why, Joseph," said James.

"Because no man is ever good enough in the eyes of a father. Remember that, Patrick, whenever you get around to asking for some unfortunate girl's hand," Joseph had a wife and daughter of his own. "Even when a father says yes his heart is saying no."

"But sure that's the sacrifice a man must make to carry on the next generation. It's not easy handing over the care of a daughter to another man," someone behind James piped up. "It's a brave man that takes on that responsibility. Especially when it comes to a McGrother woman. Is that not so, James?"

There was a chorus of laughter as the boat drew close to the shore but Patrick was left with the feeling that there was some truth in the teasing that had taken place. He hoped that James did not think he had any feelings other than friendship for Mary-Anne, and wondered how he could broach the subject with him without causing offense.

A young boy was waiting among the women as the boats came ashore and Patrick recognized him as Thomas Clarke's youngest son. Approaching James, he handed him a note with a length of green ribbon wrapped around it. James stooped down for the boy to whisper something in his ear.

Having studied the piece of paper for a minute, James looked troubled and excused himself, asking Patrick if he would help his daughter to clean and load his share of the catch into her basket.

"Maggie, will you keep an eye on Mary-Anne when ye get to town? Tell Mary she's not to worry, I'll be back tonight. There's a bit of work going repairing an old wall in Castlebellingham. It's threatening to topple over and is a danger to anyone walking by, so I had best take the ass and cart and be on my way."

"You'll run yourself ragged, James, if you keep taking on so much," Maggie shouted after her brother. "Come on now, Mary-Anne, let's get our own work done. We'll not let that father of yours put us to shame."

James knew that Mary would be asleep, along with their two youngest children. They would have no need to rouse themselves for at least another hour, so he was careful not to make the slightest noise. Lying to her did not come easy for him and Mary would know straight away if he was spinning a yarn about the broken wall.

Having taken some potatoes from the pot to bring with him, James fetched his bag of masonry tools and quietly left the house. The journey gave him time to think and prepare himself for what lay ahead. He was not one to abandon someone in need, but when it meant choosing between the safety of his family and that of a friend, James knew in his heart what his decision would be

CHAPTER TWELVE

Rose looked across the room to where her nephew sat, holding his baby securely in his arms. Her heart ached for him as he tried to smile at a woman offering him her condolences.

"He should never have insisted his parents stay away. One of them could at least be here for him, Owen. It's not right that he only has Catherine at a time like this. Look at how he clutches his child, as if she will be snatched from his grasp at any moment."

"He has us, Rose, and that's as he wished it to be. Thomas is like his father. It would cut him to the bone if he was to see the grief on his mother's face. He is barely holding out as it is. Be thankful that Catherine is here for him. She'll take care of the two of them for now."

"Aye that she will. She is as much like her mother as Thomas is the cut of his father. It's a blessing that the doctor's wife and daughter have taken a long trip to France, visiting their relatives. Catherine will not be needed until their return," said Rose.

"She fell on her feet the day you got her that position in Doctor Henshaw's house, Rose. She tells me they have even given her paid leave to be with her brother."

Owen stopped speaking at the approach of their nephew. Thomas had put a brave smile on his face that fooled neither of them.

"Could you take Eliza for a while, Aunt Rose, I need a breath of air but it's far too cold outside for her."

"I'm honoured that you'll trust me with her, Thomas. You haven't let her out of your arms all morning. I can see the other women itching to get a hold of her," said Rose.

By the time the young man reached the door to the street he had been offered condolences and sympathy by at least half a dozen young women.

"Would you look at them? Like bees around a honeypot, ready to step into a dead woman's shoes before she's even cold in her grave."

"Ah, Rose, you can't blame them. Thomas is a fine young man and a good prospect for any woman looking for a husband," said Owen.

"That may be so, but I fear that over time, loneliness may get the better of him and none of those girls would make a good mother for our wee Eliza," Rose kissed the baby's cheek. "Go on after him, love, and have a word. Find out what he intends to do after his trip to Ireland. He has not said much about his plans."

Owen caught up with his nephew and they headed for a local public house they knew would be quiet at that time of day. The two men toasted themselves in the glow of a roaring fire, staring at their drinks. Neither one was in the humour for conversation.

"I'm sorry, Owen, I'm not much company for you. I don't mind if you go back to the house."

"I'm not in form for any banter myself, son. The chatter of all those women was beginning to hurt my ears. Did you notice how many young ones came to pay their respects?" asked Owen.

"They were friends of Jane's younger sisters. If truth be told, I needed to get myself away from their pitying eyes. Is that what I have to look forward to? The pathetic young widower with a poor motherless child to care for. Why do women think, men don't know one end of a baby from the other?"

Having just taken a mouthful of porter, Owen laughed at Thomas's words and a dribble escaped from his lips. Wiping his chin, he studied his nephew's doleful face.

"Your aunt Rose is worried about you getting snared by one of those young ones. She fears as the months go by, the loneliness will become too hard to bear and you'll be looking for a mother for your wee baby. Am I safe enough in telling her she has nothing to be anxious about?"

On the other side of the room, a group of elderly men sat around a table playing cards. Every now and again a burst of laughter erupted. Thomas kept his eyes on them as he took a long drink of his ale. Wiping his top lip, he paused before answering the question his uncle had put to him.

"I've had a word with Catherine and she has agreed to travel to Ireland with me on Sunday. It will be a nice surprise for the family to find the two of us on their doorstep. They are only expecting myself and the baby. Mr. Feeney has given me a week's leave, unpaid, but he has been very generous in assisting with the funeral costs," Thomas narrowed his eyes and held his uncle's gaze. "Can you keep a secret, Uncle Owen?"

That was something the older man had plenty of practice doing from a very young age. A conversation came to mind that he overheard as a ten year old. It had taken place between his father and his uncle, concerning Pat McGrother's part in a fatal accident. Thomas's father, James, had been the only person Owen had ever revealed that secret to.

"I can, son. It's something I do very well. You can ask your father that, when you see him."

"You mustn't mention a word of what I'm about to tell you to Rose, or any of the family until I've had a chance to talk with Da about it. I know he won't like what I have to say, but I've made up my mind and there'll be no changing it."

Thomas took another mouthful of ale as Owen patiently waited.

"I'm off to America as soon as I have the fare saved. I know that Ma will take care of Eliza. It was Jane's last wish that I leave her in my parents' care when she was gone. She broached the subject with me months ago, but I refused to discuss it with her. That was wrong of me, but I couldn't bear to think about a time when I would crawl into a cold, empty bed after a long day of work at the printers. I didn't want to imagine a future without her and it was – it was the . . ."

Thomas could no longer hold back his tears. He leaned over, resting both elbows on his knees, and Owen watched silently as small, wet patches appeared on the dusty, stone floor.

"I'm sorry, I'm behaving like a child. If Jane could see me now, she would scold me for sure," said Thomas, composing himself.

"Sure isn't she looking down on you as we speak, son? Don't be making her sad by getting yourself all upset like this."

"I don't believe in all that nonsense, Owen. Jane did, that's why I had the priest say a Mass for her. But I find no comfort in religion."

"Merciful heaven, lad. Don't let your parents hear you say that. Nor your aunt Rose for that matter. I'd keep that bit of information to myself if I were you," Owen was stunned.

"Catherine knows, but nobody else in the family does. I'm sorry if I've offended you, I'm just being honest. There are a lot of things you don't know about me, Uncle Owen. I think my family are in for quite a few surprises and I hope it doesn't turn them against me."

Owen drained the last few drops of his porter and smacked his lips together.

"This is not the conversation I was expecting to have with you, Thomas. I think we had best be getting back before you reveal any more disturbing facts about yourself. I'm thankful I won't be with you when you visit your parents."

Thomas laughed as he stood up from the table, "After seeing the look of shock on *your* face, I might just keep the bit about my faith, or lack of it, to myself."

CHAPTER THIRTEEN

Inspector Armstrong was fuming. If he hadn't been called to Dublin, for a futile meeting that resolved nothing in the long run, the attack would never have been made on his barracks. With only half the usual number of men guarding the place, it was an easy target.

"They must have left some kind of a trail behind them. Are you sure that none of you saw even a glimpse of their faces. What about their dialect? What county did it sound like?"

The constables looked at each other and shook their heads. Two of them were new recruits, sent over from England and could hardly tell an Irish accent from a Scottish one, or even a Welsh one for that matter.

"You two have lived very sheltered lives haven't you? What on earth are you doing in the constabulary anyway, you should be officers in the army, judging by your fancy bearing," he spat out the words.

"It was my fault, Inspector Armstrong. I should have run back to alert the others, instead of trying to fend off those men. I only heard one of them speak, he had a Dublin accent."

"Good man, Constable Masterson. At least you tried to stop them," Armstrong noted the cuts on the other man's face and a dark patch that was forming around one of his eyes. "Thank goodness they didn't shoot you after they knocked you out," then he turned his attention to the young recruits. "As for you two, I'm sure Constable Masterson here can find plenty of work for you to attend to in this filthy rat-hole. Off with you now and leave me to write up some sort of a report that will lessen the embarrassment of your inadequacies. As far as anyone outside of these walls are concerned, it was a gang of eight men that attacked you, not five. Is that clear?"

The three constables nodded in agreement and left their superior alone, thankful that his rant was over. Henry Armstrong was annoyed that he had lost his bait. The son of someone with such a prominent position among the rebels would have been a great bargaining chip. It was futile searching for him, he felt sure that the young man was already on a boat across to England. He had no good reason to keep him detained, even though the recent suspension of *habeas corpus* allowed him to. A re-arrest would only make matters worse.

******

When James arrived at Castlebellingham he was met by a young boy who climbed up onto the cart beside him. He had recognized the green ribbon tied to the donkey's bridle. No words were exchanged except to give directions to a small farmhouse, not too far from the shoreline.

"Is that the wall yonder?" asked James as he jumped down from the cart.

"It is. Me and my brothers spent all night pulling it apart so you'd have something to repair when you got here."

A man came out from the house and shook James's hand, instructing the boy to take care of the animal. Leading him away from the cottage, towards a small stone cabin, he told James to be prepared for bad news.

"My wife is making a bit of breakfast for ye, I'll send it over with one of the boys," he opened a roughly made door. "Your friend is in here."

James's heart was racing as he peered into the dim light. The note had told him Michael Kiernan needed his help and he should go to Castlebellingham if he was willing to give it.

The sound of a man sobbing came from the gloom at the far end of the draughty, old cabin. James stepped inside calling out his friend's name.

"Is that you, Michael? Are you alone?"

Another bout of sobbing reached his ears. "It's me. It's James, can you answer me, Michael?"

The thought that it could be some sort of trap flashed through James's head and he was on the verge of turning around to make good his escape, when a familiar voice called out to him.

"You came. I wasn't sure if you would."

"Michael, are you hurt?" asked James running forward.

When he got close to where his friend sat on a bed of straw, James realized that he was not alone. A young man was lying beside him, his head resting on Michael's lap.

"This is my son, Francis. Pull that piece of wood away from the hole in the wall, James, and let a bit of light in so you can see what a fine man he turned out to be," said Michael.

Removing the piece of wood that had been wedged in place, James turned to see a shaft of weak sunlight envelope the father and son.

"The spit of me, isn't he?" Michael tried to smile as the face he tenderly stroked was illuminated.

Kneeling down on the straw, James touched the young man's forehead. It was cold as ice. He looked into Michaels red rimmed eyes before sitting opposite him, lost for words. The young face was battered and bruised and James could see no resemblance whatsoever between father and son, except for the dark, wavy hair.

"Sure he's as handsome a divil as his father is, and that's for sure," he said.

There was a knock on the door and James jumped with the fright it gave him. Michael, on the other hand, never moved an inch.

A young boy entered and nervously approached the tragic scene. He stooped to leave a tray of food on the ground in front of the men.

"I'm sorry for your trouble, sir," he said, backing away towards the open door.

"Thank your mother for us will you? Good lad," said James.

Neither of the men could eat a thing but James made his friend sip the hot tea.

"I have never felt a pain such as this in my life, James. I fear that I cannot bear it for much longer. If I hadn't sent you that note I would have used this on myself," Michael held up a pistol that had been hidden in the straw beside him.

James recoiled in horror at the sight of it. He felt sickened at the thought of what might have taken place had he ignored his friend's request for help.

"Have you taken leave of your senses, Michael? I almost didn't come, for fear that your note was a trap. It's a blessing you added the word *seashells* to it, or I might not be here now."

"Ah yes, our old password, it was an afterthought. I'm glad I remembered. I might still use this on myself, but not right now. Francis must have a decent burial. I want to lay him to rest with his grandparents, in Haggardstown," Michael stroked his son's battered face. "Will you arrange the funeral for me, James? I cannot openly attend but will find a way to be there. One of my uncles still lives in Dundalk, he'll represent me. Poor Brigid, this will break her heart."

"Do you want to tell me what happened to Francis? Or is it something you cannot discuss?" asked James.

"He was beaten to death. Isn't that obvious by the state of his face? Armstrong did it, remember him, James? They took Francis into custody as soon as he stepped off the boat in Dundalk. Word of his condition came from one of the constables guarding him. There are some even within their own ranks who are in favour of the cause."

"Why did you have him removed, Michael? Surely it would have been better to let them answer for what they did to him," said James.

"You misunderstand. He was alive and in a bad way when the men got to him but he walked out of the prison, refusing to let anyone carry him. A trusted doctor was here, waiting for Francis to arrive, but it was too late. The men who helped him to escape thought he was sleeping under the covers in the back of the cart."

Michael's voice broke and he paused briefly to compose himself.

"He was dead when we lifted him down. The doctor examined him and it was his opinion that Francis died from bleeding internally," Michael was crying once more as he smoothed down a lock of his son's hair.

For a few moments, James felt like an intruder. He was thankful that his own children had not become involved in anything subversive or illegal. It was bad enough to lose a child through accident or ill health, never mind having their life violently taken from them.

"Do you know what Armstrong would have done with my son's body, had he died in his custody?"

"No, Michael, I don't. What would he have done?"

"He would have written a false report and signed a release document for Francis. Then his men would have taken my son's body, under cover of darkness, and thrown him from a cliff-top, to be dashed onto the rocks below. It would look as if he had thrown himself over and the fall had killed him. That's what Armstrong would have done. It's happened before and he will do it again. Unless someone gives him what he deserves."

James knew what Michael was thinking and tried to dissuade him from carrying out a plan that was sure to end badly for his friend.

"Isn't one death in the family enough for Brigid and your children to cope with? If you go after Armstrong it will backfire on you, Michael. He is too well protected and you would be caught. Give me your word you will not do anything foolish."

Michael looked with sad eyes at James as he spoke about his estranged wife.

"She forbade me to have anything to do with the children as long as I was involved with the cause – and wasn't she right, James? Look at what I've done to my eldest child."

"Francis was not a child, Michael. He was a young man, capable of making up his own mind. You didn't force him to do anything. He would not be happy to hear you speak like that. Now, come away with me and get some rest."

Michael shook his head, saying he intended to spend the night with Francis's body. He repeated his request that James arrange the funeral for his son.

"I will, Michael, of course I will. I had better go out to do a bit of work on that wall now. I'll come back and see you before I head away."

James stood and placed a hand on his friend's shoulder. No words were necessary as he stepped back from the broken hearted father cradling his dead son. At the door he paused to look once more on a scene he prayed he would never find himself in. Donning his cap, James went outside to find his cart, inhaling deep into his lungs the familiar, comforting smell of the sea.

CHAPTER FOURTEEN

The water out in the bay was calm and welcoming, yet Thomas felt as if he had just rowed through a storm. His father pulled up his oars and turned to scrutinize the young man's face.

"What ails you son, too much of the porter in Paddy Mac's last night, was it?"

"No Da. I was the same on the boat coming over. I don't think I have the makings of a fisherman, do I?" laughed Thomas.

"It's a blessing that you kept up your schooling, so. Do you want to head back to shore?"

"Can we just stay here for a wee minute and not move the boat? I'll feel better if we do that," Thomas looked at the wide expanse of water around him. "It's so peaceful out here, I see now why you have always loved this place."

For a while, the two of them sat quietly surveying the scene set out before them, comfortable in their silence and lost in their own thoughts.

Looking back at the village, Thomas ran his eyes along the row of buildings that lined the shore; a mix of hotels, lodging houses and fishermen's cottages. They stood like sentries, guarding the place that was to become his daughter's home. Looking from left to right, the young man drew a line with his eyes along the gentle curve of the shore line.

"The village looks like it's smiling at us, Da. Did you ever notice that yourself?"

James immediately saw what his son was describing.

"No, I never did but I can see it now that you mention it."

"Why do ye mostly fish at night? Is it so the catch will be fresh for market?"

"Aye, that's one of the reasons. The other one is because the fish would see our nets in daylight. I should bring you out here on a moonlit night, Thomas. A man can quell his restless thoughts in the stillness of the bay," James put a hand on his son's shoulder. "Is there something you've been trying to tell me, Thomas?"

"There is, Da. You know me so well. I tried to tell you yesterday, not long after we landed on your doorstep, but Ma and the children were so excited I never got the chance."

"Sure aren't they still as excited this morning. You only have yourself to blame for that, arriving with Catherine beside you. I wish I had been there to see the look on your Ma's face," said James.

"Did you ask me to come out in the boat with you so we could have a bit of privacy?" asked Thomas.

"Son, just tell me whatever it is that's causing the constant furrows on your young brow. I know that Jane's death has been a terrible blow to you, and rightly so, but you have a wee child to think of now."

"I thought I had prepared myself for losing Jane, I knew of her sickness the day I met her. She took a part of me with her, Da and I'm no good for Eliza the way I feel now. Maybe in time it will be different but for the present I know what I must do," Thomas took a deep breath. "Jane made me promise to leave our daughter in your care. She wanted you and Ma to give her the home she knew I would be incapable of providing on my own."

"Sure we can help you, son. Your sisters and your Ma would be only too happy to care for her while you are at work. You could try the printers in town, they might have a position to offer you. I'm sure your Mr. Feeney would give you a good recommendation," James did not want his son to make a rash decision.

"No Da. I don't see Ireland as my home, not even in the future. I've been involved in the socialist movement in England for a while now. That column you used to read in Mr. Feeney's periodical, the one by R. E. Ruobal, it's me that writes it. If you spell the name backwards it says *labourer*. I came close to telling you on more than one occasion," said Thomas.

"Well now, aren't you the clever one. I'm right proud of you, son, but those words can land you in a lot of hot water. Does Mr. Feeney know it's you that writes them?"

Thomas explained that his employer had no idea who the mystery columnist was, and that Catherine was the only other person to know the truth.

"Mr. Feeney's sympathies lie with the working man but there is only so far he can go with his support," Thomas looked wistfully across the expanse of water and sighed deeply. "I lost my beautiful young wife to a sickness brought on by injurious working conditions, but there is a turning of the tide, Da, and I want to play my part in it. The working classes of the world are becoming a force to be reckoned with. They are no longer voiceless."

"I understand son but your Ma will not be so accommodating. She will berate you until the very last minute, before you go back to England, in the hopes of changing your mind. Don't fret too much about it, though. I'll remind her that you are only across the water. Sure you'll be back to see Eliza as much as you can," James picked up the oars. "We should head for home, Thomas. My stomach is telling me it needs feeding."

"I'm not going back to England, Da. I'm going to America. I have a position waiting for me on a periodical in New York. But I promise to come visit whenever I can, only I fear that will be not be very often, given the distance."

James dropped his oars as a heavy weight formed in the pit of his stomach.

"Not America, Thomas, it's too far. Can't you do the same work in England? Surely they need men like you there, too."

Thomas began to row, feeling his father's eyes upon him. He knew what he would see in them and focused instead on the horizon.

"I'm sure to end up in jail if I remain in England. America is a young country with fresh ideas, where there is more freeness of speech. R. E. Ruobal's true identity will soon be discovered, he is beginning to attract a lot of attention, from all quarters. That's how I came to be offered the work in New York," the young man stopped rowing and frowned. "Am

I to take this boat in on my own or are you going to help me?"

"Your words have taken the wind out of me, Thomas. I'm at a loss as to what I should say to you."

"Then give me your blessing and tell me you'll break the news to Ma for me, please."

James picked up his oars and with his back to his son, began to row. "I'll give you my blessing, although I'm reluctant to do so. But as far as your mother is concerned, that is something you must see to yourself. It would break my heart to give her such news. No, Thomas lad, I cannot help you with that."

CHAPTER FIFTEEN

Maggie gave a chuckle as her eyes swept from one side of the room to the other. A few of the neighbours had gathered to pay their respects to Thomas on the loss of his wife and to congratulate James and Mary on their first grandchild.

"What has you so amused, Maggie?"

"I'm not sure if I should tell you, it might cause offense. I feel as if I'm watching a play, it's better than any theatre."

Mary rolled her eyes but her curiosity was aroused. She pretended not to be interested in what her sister-in-law might be observing and didn't respond immediately. Maggie's eyes darted around the room making it difficult for Mary to pinpoint exactly who or what was the source of her amusement.

"You and your imagination, you're always seeing things that are not really happening. Go on, tell me what it's about this time. I promise not to be offended," said Mary.

Maggie looked at her with feigned disgust, "Imagination, is it now? And what about our wee Mary-Anne yonder, besotted with young Patrick? I suppose I was imagining that, was I?"

Mary shook her head and smiled. James's older sister had an uncanny knack of seeing things that others missed, even when they took place right under their noses. James had the same way about him, but he always kept it to himself.

"Well, are you going to tell me what you're looking at that's so interesting? I'm going cross-eyed trying to follow your gaze," said Mary.

Shifting in her seat as she straightened out her dress. Maggie prepared herself to point out something she felt should have been obvious to Mary.

"It was very good of Catherine to bring us these dresses, wasn't it, Mary? You look ten years younger in yours."

"Stop your dilly dallying and tell me what you're looking at?"

"Do you see the look on Mary-Anne's face?" Maggie waited for a nod of the head. "Well now, who do you think she's scowling at?"

"Why Patrick, of course. He's not paying any attention to her. But that's not unusual," observed Mary.

"Look again," said Maggie.

As she glanced from her daughter to the young man and back again, Mary was thinking that whatever Maggie saw was a figment of her imagination. Over the chatter of conversation in the small cottage, a baby's cry sounded loud and clear. Catherine was quick to turn away from the group she was in conversation with, to lift up her niece.

It was then that Mary saw what her sister-in-law had been trying to point out to her. Mary-Anne's scowl followed Catherine to the cradle and back again to where she re-joined Patrick and a young married couple expecting their first child.

"Oh Maggie, what am I to do with that girl? She's making a fool of herself over young Patrick. He's not in the least bit interested in her, he as much as told her father that yesterday."

"Oh Master Gallagher definitely has an interest in your daughter, Mary. But not in Mary-Anne. Did you not see the look on his face when he came over with me to meet Thomas and Catherine? Sure, who could blame the lad, your girl has grown up to be a fine young woman and pretty as a picture."

When Maggie turned her head to face her sister-in-law the expression on Mary's face caused her to laugh out loud. Her head was craned forward and she was squinting her eyes.

"For heaven's sake, stop making it so obvious that you're watching them. You look like a turkey blinded by the sun. Do it like this," Maggie smiled sweetly and looked around the room, her eyes resting for no more than a few seconds on the group they had been observing.

"See, Mary? That's how it's done – discreetly. Then you sweep your eyes back over them again. Like so."

James sat down beside his wife and sister announcing that the men were about to leave for Paddy Mac's, to wet the baby's head.

"That will make it a bit easier for you to watch over the goings on, Maggie," he said.

"It takes one McGrother to know another," said Mary. "Your sister has been giving me lessons."

"Sure isn't it the men being in the picture that forms the story. Without them there'd be nothing stirring. All the same, I'm mighty glad ye're going, my poor old eyes need a break from all this observing," Maggie sighed.

Thomas walked across the parlour and handed his daughter to his mother.

"Catherine is taking the younger children off to the beach for a bit of fresh air, but I fear it's too cold for Eliza. I'm away with Da and the men to Paddy Mac's – wet the baby's head and all that. We must keep up our traditions whatever else we do. Is that not so, Ma?"

CHAPTER SIXTEEN

Thomas and Patrick were deep in conversation, their heads close together as they spoke. They shared the same political views and Patrick was impressed by the maturity of the younger man. He looked over at James who seemed to be having a serious discussion with Matthew Clarke.

"You're very like your father, both in looks and in manner."

"I'll take that as a compliment, Patrick. I think that if my father had not had the responsibilities of a brood of children to care for, he would have been more active in seeking change in society," said Thomas.

"Don't be so sure of his inactivity. See how Matthew Clarke is listening to him? I've noticed the likes of him have a lot of respect for your father, Thomas. I'm only saying this so you may see James in a different light. I would trust him with my life," Patrick's hand went instinctively to the scar on his side, "And I believe every man here would be of the same opinion. That kind of trust is not earned lightly,"

Thomas took a long, hard look at the two men standing by the bar. The expression on Matthew Clarke's face was of a person showing keen interest in what was being said.

"I always took my father to be one who follows others. At this present moment he looks more like a leader," Thomas leaned forward.

James noticed his son watching him and smiled in his direction. The gesture brought an automatic response from the young man and he raised his drink high and returned the smile.

"Thomas, I was involved in a bit of trouble before I came to Ireland. Your father knows about it but I don't think he holds it against me."

Turning his attention back to his companion, Thomas questioned him about the trouble.

"A close friend of mine died because of the conditions he worked in. He was only twenty-seven years of age but he had the lungs of an old man."

"I'm sorry to hear that, Patrick. What was the nature of his employment?" asked Thomas.

"You sound like a constable, where did you learn to speak like that?"

"From books and from listening to the talk of learned men. Not that it's done me too many favours," laughed Thomas. "My mother would say it's given me 'airs and graces' and led me astray from the church."

"The last time I listened to a 'learned' man I received a knife in the side for my trouble. I took an interest in the rights of workers, because of my friend dying so young, and I attended some meetings that were causing a bit of bother for the steelworks. A gang of ruffians, sent to cause trouble, waylaid us afterwards and one of them attacked me with a knife. In the struggle he somehow ended up being stabbed with his own weapon. If it was me that did it, it was in self-defence, but my Da sent me over here with my older brother.

He was afraid someone would come looking for me."

"I imagine if that was the case you would have heard something by now," assured Thomas. "A few months ago I wrote about the history of dire working conditions in the steel industry and my employer printed it in his paper. Was your friend a grinder, by any chance?" asked Thomas.

"He was a fork grinder, but he started out as a polisher. That's part of their apprenticeship. It wasn't long before his voice turned rough and after a time his breathing became laboured."

Thomas told Patrick of a medical report he had read while doing his research. It stated that a fork grinder had the shortest life expectancy of all the grinders, the average age of death among them was twenty-nine.

"Did your friend have 'grinder's lung' and spit up blood?"

"He did, Thomas, and he shrunk in size. If he could have stood upright he would have been taller than me, but years of bending over the grinding stone gave him a curved back. You can easily pick those workers out of a crowd."

"Is that why you didn't follow your friend into the trade?"

Patrick laughed as he remembered the row he had with his father when he left school.

"I fully intended becoming an apprentice, there was plenty of work going and a decent enough wage once you'd served your time. But my father had other plans for me. We had a fierce row the day I told him I'd got myself a job in the steelworks. He marched me down to the market, where a friend of his had a fishmonger's stall, and I started that very day. I was ten years old but by the time I was eleven and had heard all those stories of the sea, I knew I wanted to be a fisherman. I got myself onto the crew of one of the boats that came upriver after that."

"That's why you've settled here so well then. You must feel right at home among the people of Blackrock," Thomas looked around Paddy Mac's as he spoke.

"They've accepted me as one of their own and I couldn't be more grateful. I would have been happy to stay here but for a recent event. Now I'm not sure what I should do."

"What event was that?"

Patrick had never been an impulsive type but the arrival of Catherine McGrother had greatly unsettled him.

"Meeting your sister, Catherine. I hope you don't take offense, Thomas, I mean no disrespect, but from the moment I laid eyes on her I have not been able to get her out of my thoughts."

"I'm not offended, Patrick, nor am I surprised. I saw how she reacted upon shaking your hand, when Maggie brought you over to meet us."

"You saw it, too? I was afraid I had imagined it. Do you think your father would mind if I paid Catherine a visit before she returns to England? I need to know if she has the same feelings for me."

"It's not my father that should concern you. I cannot see my sister leave her employment too easily, Patrick. I fear you may be in for a disappointment."

CHAPTER SEVENTEEN

Henry Armstrong was a patient man. He had learned from his father how to bide his time, while keeping himself focused on his goals. The knowledge that he would have been proud of his only son becoming a district inspector, brought a smile to the normally scowling face of the middle aged man.

An image of James McGrother invaded his thoughts and caused the corners of Armstrong's mouth to droop once more.

"I'll bide my time, McGrother. When you eventually slip up, you'll find me there ready and waiting to catch you," the district inspector said to himself.

A knock on the door announced the arrival of a report that Armstrong had been eagerly awaiting.

"So, McGrother was the one who arranged the funeral, just as I thought," Henry scanned the words on the report he had been given. "And his friend, Kiernan, was nowhere to be seen. What kind of a father does not attend his son's burial? Are you quite sure he wasn't there?"

The young constable was perspiring underneath his uniform, not from the heat but from anxiety. He had been among the large contingent of police and militia that surrounded the graveyard in Haggardstown, the day that Francis Kiernan was buried. Although he was the only one to have spotted the young man's father standing among the bearded fishermen, he never said a word. It was bad enough that he had colluded in a prisoner's escape. If it was discovered that he had turned a blind eye to the presence of Michael Kiernan among the crowd of mourners, the young constable feared that he himself would end up as a guest of her majesty for a very long time.

"Do you need me to stay on and help with that report, sir?"

Armstrong looked up from his desk, "No thank you, Masterson, you can leave now. It's been a long day."

As the door closed the district inspector congratulated himself on taking the young constable under his wing. He had been keeping a keen eye on the new recruit and saw the potential he had to rise through the ranks.

Having checked the cells before calling it a night, Constable Masterson was only too glad to get away from the stifling presence of his district inspector. It was common knowledge that Armstrong had taken a shine to the young man, making his position even more precarious. He could have done more to help the cause if he had not attracted so much uninvited attention from his superior officer.

Lately, the man had been treating him like a son and it was beginning to stab at Masterson's conscience. It was extremely difficult to be disloyal to someone who went out of his way to be so encouraging and amicable.

In the early hours of the morning, District Inspector Henry Armstrong made his way to his lodgings. Although allotted living quarters, the offer of room and board at the house of one of the local landlords was much more appealing to him.

In return, the household felt secure having someone of such a high police rank in their midst. Armstrong knew that if he had a family in tow there would have been no question of such an invitation from the gentry.

As he stepped into the kitchen a young scullery maid, who slept in a cupboard in the warm room, was just beginning her morning chores. Armstrong smiled as she gave a little curtsy, informing her there would be no need to tend the fire in his room that day.

Climbing the back stairs to his quarters, a great tiredness overcame him and the district inspector gave a deep sigh as he bent to remove his boots. He had never regretted not taking a wife from among the few women he had been attracted to over the years, but the absence of a son in his life had bothered him of late.

There was something about Masterson that touched a chord with him. It was what had influenced Armstrong to take the young constable under his wing. As he eased himself between the crisp, starched sheets, Henry Armstrong congratulated himself on being a good judge of character.

Stepping out from under the cover of an old drooping willow tree, Michael Kiernan watched the lights dim in the third floor window of the big house. It was worth the risk of being discovered to have followed the middle aged inspector home to his lodgings. Michael had been on his tail for over a week and gathered enough information about the man to put into motion the next stage of his plan.

As he climbed over the high wall surrounding the landlord's estate, Michael gave one last look back at the window he had been observing. "I have you now, Armstrong," he whispered. "I have you now."

CHAPTER EIGHTEEN

Catherine looked again at the note that had been slipped into her pocket by the cook earlier that morning. Her mistress was nursing a bad cold and had taken to her bed, instructing Catherine to mend a tear in one of her dresses.

Even though the young woman had become accustomed to receiving such correspondence, each time a piece of paper was produced by the cook it made her heart race. At first, Catherine had tried to ignore the young man, feigning disinterest in his attention. Only the cook knew about the perseverance he displayed, where other young men would have given up long before.

Aware of the fact that the sender of those notes was quite illiterate, Catherine wondered whose hand had written down the words. It felt to her as if someone was eavesdropping on their correspondence, although she had yet to reply to any of it herself.

"I might give an answer this time," she thought as she rummaged through her sewing box.

******

Patrick Gallagher checked that none of the dust from the quarry had remained on his good suit. He had left it hanging on the door of the bedroom he shared with two fellow quarrymen and they had carelessly hung their old, grubby work jackets over it the night before.

Having left the church just before Mass had ended, Patrick waited outside while the crowd filed out. As soon as he caught sight of Catherine McGrother he stepped forward and grabbed hold of her gloved hand, pulling her from the throng of people. The young woman smiled shyly, accompanying him as they made their way towards Mowbray Park. She had brought a small picnic and Patrick's eyes lit up at the site of delicacies he had never before tasted.

"Would this be your usual lunchtime fare?" he asked, his mouth full of pastry.

Catherine laughed and shook her head, "Not at all, Cook is merely showing off. She'll be pleased as punch when I describe the look of pleasure on your face. I didn't know it was possible to smile that much with a mouthful of food."

At ease in each other's company, they spent the afternoon walking around the park, sharing their hopes and dreams.

"Seeing as we're dressed in our best finery, it would be a shame not to go to the Palatine for some tea," said Patrick.

"Oh, I would love to. My brother, Thomas, used to bring me there, for a treat."

"I know he did. In fact, he told me that should I ever convince you to spend time in my company, that's where I must take you," Patrick replied. "How is your brother faring in America? Well, I hope."

"Very well indeed, thank you for asking. I received a letter from him just this week."

Having finished their afternoon tea in the elegant surroundings of The Palatine Hotel, they returned to where they had shared the picnic. The weather being so nice, the rest of the day was spent in Mowbray Extension Park. The new section had been recently opened, with a lake and terrace being added. The young couple had agreed that if they ran into any of the McGrothers, Catherine would introduce Patrick as an old friend of her brother's, who was thinking of joining him in America.

As they walked across the newly erected footbridge towards the older section of the park, Patrick felt that the year 1866 would be a pivotal one in his life. He resolved in his heart to do all in his power to convince the young woman by his side to marry him.

"Does my father know that you are here?" Catherine's voice interrupted his thoughts and Patrick had to ask that she repeat her question.

"I thought it best not to tell him, after his absolute refusal to allow me to court you. He thinks I've gone to Liverpool instead. You're aunt Maggie knows where I am though. It was her idea that I look for work in Sunderland. She said not to tell the rest of the family just yet."

Catherine laughed as she remembered the look on Patrick's face the day he asked her father's permission to call on her. She had been sitting at the table and had refused to leave the room, allowing the men to speak in private. Patrick had called thinking she had accompanied her mother and younger siblings to the beach and that James was alone in the house.

Her father's immediate and absolute refusal to allow Patrick to call on her shocked Catherine. She had assumed there would be the obligatory resistance at first but then he would accede to the request. She had not heard her father speak any ill of Patrick and was under the impression that he valued the young man's friendship.

"May I ask you a question? I pray you will answer it truthfully," said Catherine, linking her arm through his.

Patrick nodded but felt his heart pound in his chest. He knew what was coming and had already decided to be honest with her.

"Why is my father so against us being together? It cannot be on account of your livelihood, for he is a fisherman himself."

Patrick steered Catherine to a wooden bench and sat beside her. Looking around to make sure nobody was close enough to see, he reached underneath his jacket and pulled up his shirt. A large white scar ran across his side and Catherine gasped at the sight of it.

"What has that got to do with my father?"

Patrick again checked there was no one within earshot, before recounting the story that led to his arrival in Blackrock.

"Although your father has never admitted this to be the reason he will not agree to our courtship, I know that it is. He's afraid one day it will catch up with me and I cannot blame him."

"Well let's not worry too much about my father's fears for now. If you would like to meet me next Sunday after Mass I would be happy to have tea with you again."

Patrick could not believe what he was hearing.

The young couple parted company at the beginning of a row of large detached townhouses. Catherine could feel Patrick's eyes watching her as she walked along the quiet street. Just before opening the gate that led to the side entrance of Doctor Henshaw's residence, she turned and waved at Patrick, not surprised to see him standing, cap in hand, smiling back at her.

"You're cutting it fine, my girl. Mr. Briggs just asked me no more than five minutes ago if everyone was accounted for," the cook chided. "By the look on your face I'd say Miss Eleanor will be looking for a new ladies maid before long."

Catherine sighed contentedly as she ate the portion of thick soup that had been saved for her, "She may have to indeed. But sure, its early days yet, Cook. I'm in no rush to get wed."

"And rightly so, young lady, rightly so. Men are nothing but a heap of trouble, mark my words. Play with them all you like but never get wed, that's what I say. Well I'm off to my bed and you had best be doing the same before old Briggs finishes his rounds."

"Goodnight, Cook. I won't be long after you."

As soon as she had emptied her bowl and washed it, Catherine took a candle to light her way up to the female servants' quarters on the third floor. Both the stairwell and long corridor to her room were windowless. During the day, when everyone was at their work, the bedroom doors were usually left open, allowing natural light into the corridor. Catherine knew at such a late hour in the evening that everyone would be in their quarters, if not in bed.

As she made her way to her room, an uneasy feeling flooded through her and she turned at the top of the stairs to glance into the shadows.

Catherine caught her breath at the sound of the lower steps creaking, and lifted high the candle she had taken from the kitchen.

"Is there anybody there?" she called softly into the darkness.

No reply came back to her. Feeling silly for being anxious over nothing, Catherine ran the full length of the long narrow hallway towards a door at the end. It belonged to the tiny room she had all to herself, which caused some envy among the female staff.

Breathing a sigh of relief, Catherine turned to close the door and was taken by surprise as the flame of the candle suddenly went out. Presuming a draught from the window must have caused it, she pushed the door forward until it was shut tight.

As she turned towards her bed the door creaked open behind her. Catherine spun around and a large hand closed over her mouth. By the size of the person dragging her into the centre of the room, she knew it was a man – a very strong man.

The room was in darkness, as the maids took it in turns to close all the bedroom shutters once the evening drew in, to conserve the day's heat. Both of them stumbled across the floor, tripping over a rag rug to land on the bed. The heaviness of the body lying on top of her was so suffocating that for a moment Catherine lay still, trying to catch her breath and make sense of the situation.

There was an overpowering scent of men's cologne, a blend that the young woman had not encountered before. Whoever this person was, they did not belong to the household. It was possible that they had followed her in from the street and hidden in wait.

Gathering every ounce of strength she could muster, Catherine punched with all her might, catching her assailant by surprise. She wriggled out from under him and slid down onto the floor, crawling on her hands and knees towards the doorway.

Just as she reached it both of her ankles were grabbed in a vice-like grip and Catherine was dragged backwards like a sack of coal. That was when she realized she had not screamed, not even once, so intent was she on escape.

As she drew a deep breath to make sure her voice would carry, a pungent, damp cloth was placed over her face, causing her to weaken and feel faint. She was picked up and thrown onto the bed as the sickening cologne enveloped her once more, mingling with the smell of chloroform. Just before consciousness left her, Catherine reached up through a darkening haze towards the shaded outline of the man's face until her hand connected with his skin. Digging her fingernails deep into a fleshy cheek was the last thing the terrified young woman remembered before passing out.

CHAPTER NINETEEN

An urgent knocking dragged Catherine from a fitful sleep and as she raised herself up, a sharp pain shot through her neck. A young kitchen maid stuck her head into the room and informed Catherine that she had missed breakfast and her mistress was looking for her.

"I must have caught her fever," Catherine said weakly. "Could you please tell Mistress Eleanor that I'll be with her shortly?"

"You sound fairly shook, alright. Shall I open the window and let some air in?"

"No. Please don't do that. Hurry now, the mistress will be waiting," said Catherine.

Through the gaps in the shutters, thin slivers of sunlight filled the room. The memories of what had taken place the night before had been seared into Catherine's mind. Even the scent of the intruder's pungent cologne seemed to hang in the air, stifling her breathing.

On easing herself out of the bed Catherine found that she was still fully clothed, though somewhat dishevelled. Every muscle she had ached and it was difficult to turn her neck from side to side. From what her body was telling her, she instinctively knew what must have happened after she had passed out, but dismissed the thought immediately from her head.

"I feared that I would never see the light of day again," she whispered, opening the painted wooden shutters.

The light streamed in and warm rays washed over her as Catherine stood quite still, offering a prayer of gratitude that she was still alive. Noticing some rips in her clothing as she undressed, Catherine consoled herself with the fact that they were nothing she could not mend. Before putting on her uniform she scrubbed every inch of her body with a rough flannel and soapy water, until there was no longer any trace of the sickening stench of cologne.

Once she had checked in on her sleeping mistress, Catherine made her way to the breakfast room to inform the family about their daughter's condition. She noticed they had guests seated at the table with them.

"Mistress Eleanor feels cool to the touch this morning, so it appears the fever has left her. Begging your pardon, sir, you being a doctor and all that."

The master laughed, assuring Catherine he had taken no offense and thanked her for the care she was giving to his daughter.

It crossed her mind to tell Doctor Henshaw of the previous night's traumatic event. He was a God-fearing man and would be outraged that such an assault could take place under his own roof. The female quarters were positioned well away from the male servants' rooms, with a locked door between the corridors.

"Before you go Catherine, do tell us what part of Ireland you hail from. Is it near Dublin?" Doctor Henshaw's voice cut into her thoughts.

"No sir, I come from a fishing village near Dundalk."

"Oh yes, I remember now. My new colleague here, Doctor Gilmore, and his good wife, have come over from Dublin to take up residence just three doors up the street. They will be staying here as our guests until their house is in order," the master smiled at his breakfast companions. "You may go now, Catherine. Please encourage Mistress Eleanor to take some chicken broth. She needs to rebuild her strength. You look quite pale yourself, my dear. Use the main stairs for today, it will not be so tiring for you," he said.

An hour later Catherine was climbing the stairs carrying a tray to her mistress's chambers when a familiar odour set her heart pounding with fear. Spinning around she came face to face with one of the house-guests she had been introduced to earlier. As he passed her by, turning his face towards her, Catherine saw two distinct scratch marks on his left cheek. Her legs weakened with shock and buckled beneath her.

The sound of the wooden tray clattering onto the tiled floor brought the butler and the master into the main hallway.

"She collapsed, poor thing, I fear she may have caught your daughter's illness. If you will send one of the servants to lead me to her quarters I shall see to it she is made comfortable," assured the visiting doctor.

"We must keep her isolated from the rest of the staff until we are sure of her condition," Doctor Henshaw advised the butler. "The last thing we need is a houseful of bedridden servants."

Once Catherine had been laid on her bed with a cold compress placed across her forehead, she began to come round. The face looking down upon her wore a menacing grimace, the eyes full of lust.

"I've sent the maid to fetch you some of that nice broth you were bringing to your sick mistress, before you fainted, my dear."

The impulse to run was so great, Catherine jumped up from the bed in one swift movement, only to be caught by the doctor and pushed back down again.

"*Alice, ALICE,*" she managed to scream before a large hand was clamped over her mouth.

"No need to alarm the rest of the servants, now, is there? I fear you may be delirious. Have you had any unsettling dreams of late? Have you been imagining all sorts of fearful events that would scare the life out of such an innocent maiden as yourself?" taunted Gilmore.

Returning with the broth, the maid almost dropped the tray at the sight of Catherine slapping the doctor across the face. It was done with such force, his head spun to the side.

Aware of her presence, the doctor assured the young girl that Catherine had been overcome by a fit of delirium. The wild eyes of his patient, fighting against his restraining grasp appeared to support the diagnoses.

"She needs plenty of rest," he released his grip, gesturing for the maid to leave the room.

"I will make sure that no one disturbs you my dear," he sneered at Catherine, as he slowly walked backwards into the hallway.

She waited until his smug expression disappeared behind the closing door before leaving her bed and staggering towards the washstand. Grabbing a ceramic basin from under its matching jug, Catherine heaved until it felt as if her stomach would be next to come up. When the waves of nausea subsided, painful sobs erupted from deep inside her and Catherine didn't even try to suppress them. Stressed and exhausted from her ordeal, she fell asleep sitting on the floor, holding the basin on her lap.

CHAPTER TWENTY

"What do you mean she's left her employment? Why would she do that?" Patrick was shocked.

Catherine had not turned up for Mass the previous Sunday and he had assumed she was ill, but when a second Sunday went by with no sign of her, he feared she had changed her mind about their relationship.

"I don't know, I told her she was being impulsive but the girl was homesick and that was that. Even Mistress Eleanor, weeping and wailing about losing her best friend, couldn't change her mind," said the cook.

"Can you please give me her address then?"

I'm not sure of the street, but it's somewhere in Bishopwearmouth, and I had best not ask the master. He's quite annoyed at the suddenness of that young woman's departure. Could you not enquire of your pastor, at that church where you met up?"

"Priest, we call him a priest, ma'am. Yes, of course. That would be the sensible thing to do. Thank you very much," he put on his cap as he walked away.

"*Better still*," thought Patrick, "*I'll call to the infirmary where Rose McGrother works.*"

It wasn't long before the hospital on Chester Road loomed before him and Patrick was quick to find a porter who knew Catherine's aunt. As luck would have it, she had been called in the night before and was just about to go off duty.

"You're the young man our Catherine had tea with, aren't you? She said you brought her to The Palatine," said Rose.

Patrick nodded and apologized for not meeting them sooner, then told her that James McGrother did not want him to have anything to do with his daughter.

"I was worried when she didn't turn up at Mass for two Sundays in a row. I was afraid your brother had found out about our meeting and had forbidden her to see me, so I called to the doctor's house. It was the cook told me she had left. Is Catherine unwell?

"She doesn't appear to be, but there is something bothering her and she refuses to talk about it. It may be that she does not want to go against her father's wishes, but that girl is like her mother. She makes up her own mind," Rose looked the young man up and down. "You might as well come back to our place. Maybe you can talk some sense into the girl, she won't listen to anything I have to say."

"Is Catherine looking for work? I might know of a place she could try," said Patrick.

"She hasn't left the house since she arrived on our doorstep. All she does is wash everything in sight from morning till evening, then falls exhausted into bed. I'm happy to come home to a house that shines like a new pin but her constant scrubbing is beginning to unnerve me. Did you two have a falling out over something?"

Patrick shook his head and told Rose he was equally as puzzled about Catherine's behaviour. They continued the rest of their journey in silence.

"Catherine, there's someone here would like a word with you," Rose called out as she stepped inside the house."

The young woman hesitated but Rose took a coat from behind the door and draped it across Catherine's shoulders. "There's a wee bit of a chill in the air. Come on outside and have a word with this young man. I think you owe him that much, at least."

Pushing her niece towards the open door she called out to Patrick. As his form appeared in the doorframe Catherine shrank back against her aunt and Rose could feel her body go rigid. Thinking Patrick had tricked her into feeling sorry for him, she pulled the frightened young woman inside and stood in front of her.

"What have you done to my niece that has her so on edge at the sight of you? You had better tell me the truth or I'll fetch her two uncle's, and they'll beat the living daylights out of you."

Catherine, who was unable to look Patrick in the eye, pulled her aunt back.

"Leave him be, Rose. He's done nothing wrong. I have hated living in the doctor's house for years, but never complained. The other maids are all jealous of me and because of that I have no friends. It's the loneliness that has driven me back home."

Catherine turned to speak to the confused young man on the doorstep, who anxiously twisting his cap in his hands.

"I'm sorry, Patrick. It would be best if you took your leave now. Please don't call again, I have nothing to offer you, not even friendship. I hope you will forgive me if I have somehow given you the wrong impression," she almost wept at the hurt etched into his face.

Rose was so taken aback at her niece's words, it took a few seconds for her to realize Catherine had closed the door, leaving Patrick confused and rejected, on the other side.

CHAPTER TWENTY-ONE

Mary smiled as the sound of a baby's laughter filled the house. She was preparing a rare meal of cooked chicken and the children were stuck indoors on account of a heavy rain that had been falling since early morning. Breege was bouncing her little niece upon her lap, while Jamie tickled her with one of the hen's feathers.

"I'm the one making her laugh, not you," said Jamie.

"No you're not. She always does this when I bounce her on my knee. Take that dirty feather away from her face. Ma, tell Jamie to stop pestering Eliza," Breege appealed to her mother.

"Stop what you're doing, the pair of ye, or she'll bring her breakfast up," said Mary.

James looked at the rain beating against the window and sighed, resigning himself to the fact it was down for the day. There would be no fishing that night, with a wind that was gathering strength.

Mary sensed his uneasiness at being trapped in the house and asked if he could repair a loosened leg on the chair by the fireplace. She had been making a list in her head of all the jobs that needed doing before their visitor arrived the following month.

"I cannot believe that Bridget Kiernan is coming to see us, after all this time. Can you, James? Read me the letter again."

"You must know it by heart, Mary, you've had me read it so often," James looked at his wife and laughed. "There's no need to give me that begging face. I'll read it again."

The children gathered around the table to hear, once more, the news from America. To them, the letter had heralded the arrival of sweets and strange knick-knacks that usually accompanied a visitor from across the Atlantic. To their parents it was a more sobering affair. Their old friend was coming to grieve for her son.

"Poor woman, I cannot imagine what she must be feeling on that voyage over, and travelling unaccompanied at that," Mary said when James had finished reading. "Surely herself and Michael can put their differences aside. They need to be together at a time like this."

James glanced at the children, who had turned their attention back to the baby. He leaned in close to his wife as she hovered over the chicken.

"Mary, you know full well the reason they cannot do that. This is not something we should discuss in front of the children," James whispered.

"I know, and I promise not to bring it up whilst Bridget is here – unless she speaks of it first, of course," Mary replied in a hushed voice, drawing even closer to James.

"Do the two of ye have a secret ye can't share with us?" their son asked.

"We were just saying a wee prayer over the poor old hen before she goes into the pot," said Mary.

"She was a good layer and will be sorely missed," added James. "Promise me ye won't let your mammy put me in the pot when I get too old to mend walls or go out in a boat."

"You'll be safe enough as long as you keep laying the eggs, Da," piped up young Jamie.

The parlour rang with laughter as James picked up his son and turning him upside down, pretended to put him into the pot with the chicken.

Later that night, when the house was quiet, James crossed the parlour to climb into the bed at the side of the fireplace. He had fixed thick posts on each corner and Mary had draped fabric around them, to offer a little privacy. James tried not to disturb his sleeping wife as he settled in beside her, but she turned instinctively as soon as she felt the movement and melted into her usual position next to him.

James remembered something from the Bible, where it talked of a man and a woman becoming 'one flesh' and drew Mary even closer.

"Maybe this is how a woman feels when she gives birth," James said to himself.

"When who gives birth?" came a sleepy question.

"I'm sorry, love, did I wake you?"

"Sure I always know when you get in beside me, even when I'm in a deep sleep. Who gave birth, James?"

"You'll think me foolish if I tell you," he answered.

"Let me be the judge of that. Tell me, or I shall be awake all night and you'll pay dearly for it in the morning," teased Mary.

"I was wondering if a mother felt the same bond for her husband as she did for her children. What do you say to that, now?" asked James.

Mary was silent for a few moments and James was relieved she had not made fun of him.

"What has you so maudlin? Would it be Bridget's visit?" asked Mary.

"Aye, I suppose it has me thinking of how she might be feeling, I saw how distressed Michael was at the loss of his son and I cannot imagine a person in more pain than that."

Mary sat up so abruptly James followed suit. As they faced each other in the darkness, she reached out a hand to touch her husband's face.

"I had a feeling you and Michael had met up, but I knew better than to ask. It surely broke his heart not to come to his own son's funeral. That poor boy had neither mother nor father to bury him. I daresay it's a blessing that Michael Kiernan has returned to America, for his wife's sake. I would not like to see their paths cross just now." Mary lay back down again.

"If you had to choose between me and the children, who would it be, Mary?" James asked the question even though he knew the answer.

"Why the children, of course. I won't lie to you James, if I am ever forced to choose between ye that would be my decision."

James was very quiet and Mary felt she may have hurt his feelings with her candid reply.

"It doesn't mean I love you any less than them. In fact, I love you more. I think, if I am to be truthful, it is a case of the greater need," she added.

Those words, spoken in the darkness, were like a revelation to James.

"Now I think I understand what that bond is like. The children need you, so of course you would choose them over me. It must have been the same for Bridget, when she asked Michael to leave the house, for the safety of the children. Do you think she still loves him, Mary?"

"She must resent the fact that he chose the Fenians over his family. I know I would, so I don't believe she still has the same feelings for him. Now, can we please get to sleep before the cockerel begins to crow?"

Mary nestled into her husband's arms as he lay down beside her but just as sleep was about to overtake her, his voice whispered in her ear.

"Do you not want to know what my choice would be, Mary? You never asked."

"I already know, James. You would choose me over the children. It would break your heart but in the end that is the decision you would make. Is that not so?"

A deep sigh told Mary it was. James kissed the top of her head and smiled.

"Yes, my love. I cannot imagine my life without you. I hope that God in his mercy will take me before he takes you and that's the truth of it, Mary. I need you more than I need the children, and they need you more than they need me. You have a knack of seeing things for what they are. I'll let you sleep now. Goodnight, love."

Mary kissed his bearded face and sighed with relief, knowing he would sleep easy that night. Had that conversation not taken place, she knew her husband would have tossed and turned until the morning, with all sorts of thoughts racing through his head.

"Goodnight, my love," whispered Mary.

She slipped into a peaceful sleep herself, happy that she had not fully explained what she meant by 'the greater need' and relieved that James had come to his own wrong conclusion about it. The truth was, Mary had a far greater need of the children than they had of her.

CHAPTER TWENTY-TWO

Rose climbed the stairs carrying a small tray. She had sent Catherine back up to bed after the young woman suffered a prolonged bout of vomiting.

"Here you are, my love. A nice cup of tea will ease your stomach. I'll be here for the day, so if you need me, just give a call."

Before leaving the room, Rose turned around and blurted out what had been on her mind as she listened to her niece vomiting for two days in a row.

"Did Patrick ever lay a hand on you? Tell me truthfully, I won't breathe a word of it to anyone."

Catherine was shocked at the forthrightness of her aunt.

"No, no he did not. Please stop asking me about him. It has been three weeks since I last laid eyes on him and I have managed to put him out of my mind."

"So you still care for him. Then why not let him visit? The lad has done nothing wrong has he? Is it because your father doesn't approve? Sure James will always have a tight hold of his children but he'll come round in the end."

Mary reached out for the basin by her side and heaved into it once more. The watery tea-coloured bile reminded Rose of her last pregnancy. Although it had been many years before, she would never forget the sickness she felt and how it drained her.

"Is there any chance that you could be with child, Catherine?"

The question flew across the room like a spear and the young woman felt as if she had been impaled. A knot took hold of her stomach and she doubled over with a loud cry.

"What is it, Catherine? Are you in pain? Do you need a doctor?" Rose was by her side in two strides.

Shaking her head, Catherine told her aunt what had taken place five weeks previously. The young woman revealed her fearful thoughts that the worst had happened while she was unconscious. She had been trying with great difficulty to forget the terrifying experience.

"I cannot bear to bring that awful night to mind, Rose," Catherine spoke between sobs. "Do you see now why it would be impossible for me to have anything to do with Patrick? If I am with child it would be unfair to him, for it's not his offspring I'm carrying."

"Do you have any clue as to who your assailant was? Think, Catherine. They should be punished for what they have done to you," Rose was fighting to control her rage against the unknown man.

Catherine shook her head, "The room was dark and I couldn't see his face. He must have sneaked into the house behind me when I entered that evening."

The young woman had sworn to herself she would never reveal the name of her attacker, not even to her aunt. Her father and his brothers would kill him for sure and end up on the gallows. It was one thing to take revenge on a man of their own class but an entirely different matter when gentry were involved.

"Are you sure that Patrick did not follow you into the house, unbeknownst to you? Could it have been he that lay in wait for you?" asked Rose.

"I know it was not Patrick. He would never do such a vile thing. Besides, this man was of a larger frame. Oh Rose, what am I to do. This will break my father's heart and my mother will be so ashamed of me."

"Don't speak such nonsense. They would never put the blame on you. Try and get some rest while I go downstairs and think about this. Between us, we will come up with a way of telling them, don't fret over it, my love."

Rose kissed her niece on the forehead and left the room. A plan was already forming in her mind, an easy one to set in motion. The difficulty would be in convincing Catherine to go along with it.

CHAPTER TWENTY-THREE

"You're very late, Rose. I'm thankful you told me to walk home ahead of you. What manner of conversation with a priest would take till this hour?" asked Owen.

Rose made up an excuse about arranging a call on a sick patient at the hospital.

"Ah sure you know how the priests love to hear the latest gossip. I had to drag myself away from him. Did you get a bit of stew from the pot, love?"

Owen nodded, complaining about having to eat alone on a Sunday. All of their children had grown up and left home. The only other person in the house with them was Catherine, and she spent most of her time in her room.

"Has she had any herself?" Rose looked up at the ceiling.

"I shouted out for her to come down and have some as soon as I returned from Mass, but there hasn't been a stir out of her. What are we going to do with the girl, Rose? Do you not think we should send her home to her parents?"

"No, that would be the wrong thing to do, Owen. James and Mary have their hands full as it is, what with a grandchild to care for along with their own brood. Give Catherine a wee bit more time. One more month, that's all. Then we'll do something if things have not changed."

"That's all I can give it, Rose. One month. If she gets any worse, James will never forgive me for keeping it from him," Owen put on his cap and jacket. "I'm off to the Peacock with

Peter. He's been commenting on how odd our Catherine has been of late and says she belongs with her parents. I'll tell him she may be joining them in a month, so."

Rose had lost her appetite for the stew she had left cooking on the stove since early morning. After removing her shawl and bonnet, she climbed the stairs with a tray for Catherine.

"Don't tell me you're not hungry or that you want to be left alone. I have news for you, so sit up and heed what I have to say, girl."

Catherine sat bolt upright and meekly took the tray from her aunt. Rose waited until half the bowl had been emptied before speaking, as she feared what she was about to reveal might put Catherine off her food.

"Do you think that Patrick would be willing to marry you?"

"I would never expect that of him, Rose. Why should he take on another man's child?"

"I told him this morning that you are missing him sorely but you feel torn between your father and himself. I've invited him over for dinner next week after Mass. You should have seen the smile on his face."

"Why did you do that without asking me first?" Catherine was horrified.

"Because you would have begged me not to. This way the deed has already been done and you cannot back out," said Rose. "On no account are you to mention what happened to you, or about the baby. I am the only one besides yourself that is privy to your condition. We must tell no one. Do you hear me, girl? No one."

Catherine nodded slowly, relieved that someone else was taking control of her situation. She was full of guilt at the thought of misleading Patrick, but as she listened to Rose speak of her plan, it became easier to accept.

******

Owen acknowledged that Patrick Gallagher had been like a tonic to his niece since they had been spending time together but he was outraged at their elopement.

"Is there any reason why you were in such a hurry to wed?" Owen glared at Patrick.

The young man held his gaze, for he had nothing to be ashamed of.

"Uncle Owen, how could you even think such a thing? Patrick has been the perfect gentleman. It was I who chose the date. September is a fine month for a marriage," Catherine took hold of Patrick's hand and glanced across the table at her aunt. "As Rose has already said, I was afraid my father would make things difficult for us. I don't expect you to give us your blessing, but there is nothing you can do about it now."

Catherine and Patrick had obtained a Registrar's Licence, which was expensive but allowed them to marry quickly and without the need for Banns to be read. Nobody but Rose and the priest who married them, knew in advance of their secret ceremony, with one of Patrick's workmates and his wife standing in as witnesses.

The young man's heart was fit to burst, he was that enraptured with his new bride.

Sadly, it wouldn't be long before a different condition of the heart took hold of Patrick, causing discomfort for more than just the newly married couple.

CHAPTER TWENTY-FOUR

Constable Masterson was relieved that the latest piece of information he had passed on, had prevented what could have been a disastrous outcome. The leader of one of the Fenian circles had been grateful for the tip off, cancelling a raid on the local militia. Police informers had alerted Masterson's district inspector to the impending attack and they were well prepared.

"Those rebel miscreants are getting too big for their boots," snarled Armstrong, stabbing his meat with a knife. "Who do they think they are, sending raiding parties into Canada? President Johnson himself has called them *'evil-disposed persons'* did you know that, Masterson?"

The young constable shook his head while continuing to eat his food. He knew that he was not expected to participate in what was more of a speech than a conversation. If putting up with the inspector's rant was the price he had to pay for a fine dinner in a fancy restaurant, then Constable Masterson was willing to give the occasional nod of the head. The assault on his ears was a fair exchange for a change of menu. The meals at the barracks had not been the best, of late.

"Even their own clergy are against them. Their Church has disowned them and their people are suffering because of misguided loyalties. They only have themselves to blame for the suspension of *habeas corpus* and I for one will make the most of that. A man will confess to anything once we can hold him indefinitely."

On and on the inspector went, until all three courses of the meal had been served up and they were the last two people left in the restaurant. Armstrong glanced around him, then leaned forward in a conspiratorial manner.

"I have reason to believe that Michael Kiernan's old pal, McGrother, may not be as disinterested in politics as he makes out. Did you know that it was he who arranged the son's funeral?"

"Yes, sir. You shared that information with me last week, but arranging a funeral does not prove an affiliation with an organization."

"I do not need the proof," snarled Armstrong. "I know it to be true. One of these days McGrother will take a false step that will lead to his downfall, and I will be there, waiting. Mark my words, Masterson. Mark my words."

Wiping his mouth with a monogrammed napkin, the young constable noticed that the staff were standing along the wall, waiting to clear the last table of the evening.

"That was a very satisfying meal, thank you, District Inspector Armstrong," Masterson gave the man his full title. "Do you think we might finish up now and allow the waiters to get on with their work? All the other diners have left the premises."

As he settled the bill, Armstrong instructed the head waiter to order a hansom cab. On the short journey to the barracks Constable Masterson used the brandy induced camaraderie between them to seek out a piece of sensitive information.

"With regard to that rebel scum, Michael Kiernan, is there any evidence to prove he has definitely left the country?" asked Masterson.

"Indeed there is, young man. He was identified by those worthless documents he is so quick to wave in the face of British authority. Two days after crossing from Drogheda to Liverpool, he boarded a ship bound for New York, but do not think for one minute that we have seen the last of Kiernan. We have our spies in the shipping offices who will know the minute he books a ticket to sail back this way. I can guarantee he will return and we both know of one man in particular who is bound to receive a visit from him, do we not?"

Constable Masterson nodded his head in agreement and wondered why the man sitting opposite him nursed such a grudge against a village fisherman. There had been no evidence produced of any illegal activity whatsoever on the part of James McGrother, nor any of his relatives in Ireland or England. No matter how many people Armstrong questioned nothing ever incriminated him or any member of his family. Masterson felt the constant surveillance to be a complete waste of time and energy.

"If there is any threat to Kiernan or McGrother I will be the first to warn them," thought Masterson. *"And I am not the only constable in Ireland whose sympathies lie where District Inspector Armstrong least expects them to."*

CHAPTER TWENTY-FIVE

The document sat accusingly on the table between them. Patrick had taken it from a box where he kept all of his personal possessions. It had been there for exactly one month, lying on top of his bone handled fishing knife. He rubbed his calloused palms together, wishing the hard skin could have come from the oars of a boat instead of a pick and shovel.

"Can you read the words out to me, Catherine? We have never really looked at it before," said Patrick.

Sliding their marriage certificate across the well-scrubbed table top, to a position where she could read it easily without picking it up, Catherine felt as though she had committed a crime. She could barely stand to look at the evidence, let alone touch it.

"Please read it to me, I need to hear what it says," Patrick spoke in a low, even tone.

Catherine's voice was barely above a whisper as she read aloud the neatly scripted words.

"Your name is on it and your age is twenty-four. *Bachelor*. Your rank or profession is *quarry labourer* and then the address at *Farrington Row*. Your father is *Thomas Gallagher*," Catherine paused before reading the next two words, "*Gardener. Deceased.*"

"It feels like he's been gone a lot longer than a few months. Please continue," said Patrick.

"Then my name, age twenty-two, *spinster*,"

"Hah," interrupted Patrick, leaning forward. "The first lie. But a necessary one, I'll give you that. If it was known you are not yet twenty-one, we would have needed your father's permission. Please continue," the chair creaked as he sat back into it.

Catherine nervously cleared her throat, "The address here is written down. My father's name, *James McGrother, Fisherman.* At the bottom are the names of the witnesses and our own names."

"And there we have the second lie," Patrick stood up. "Why did you put your mark on the register when you are well able to write? Does it make you feel less married to have made two small strokes of ink instead of writing your name in your own hand?"

Patrick had moved around the table and grasped his wife by the shoulders, pulling her up from the chair.

"No, Patrick. That's not why I did it," Catherine cried. "I didn't want to embarrass you or your friends, by being the only one among us who could write. Please let go, you're frightening me."

Pushing her back down onto the chair, Patrick walked towards the door and took his cap and jacket from a hook, without sending a glance or a word across the room to his wife. Owen and Rose had left the house earlier to give them some privacy and as Patrick slammed the door behind him, Catherine lay her head and arms on the table and wept.

An hour later she was still in the same position when she heard Rose's voice outside, passing by the window. Before the couple stepped through the door, Catherine had jumped up to stand at the stove, with her back to them. She knew her eyes would be red and swollen from an hour of crying and made an excuse of being tired as she inched her way towards the stairs, without turning around to face them.

"I'll bring you up a cup of tea, love. Has Patrick gone out?" asked Rose.

"He'll be up there waiting for his wife if he's worth his salt," teased Owen.

Catherine let out a loud sob and raced up the steps to the room she had shared with Patrick since their wedding day.

Rose glared at her husband, before following their niece up the stairs.

"What did I do, now?" he shouted after her. "Women! A man can't open his mouth for fear of offending or upsetting them."

Catherine did not reply to the knock on her door, so Rose slowly opened it, even though she was sure that Patrick was not in the room.

"Did you two have another disagreement?" she asked, sitting on the edge of the bed.

"He was really angry this time. He even accused me of lying to him," sobbed Catherine.

"Oh no. Has he discovered you are with child?"

As her niece turned to face her, Rose was taken aback at the puffiness in her face and her red-rimmed eyes. She took a flannel from the wash stand and dipped it into some cool water.

"Here you are, girl. Press this against those swollen eyes. You don't want your husband to come back to a face like that, do you?"

"He doesn't know about the baby, Aunt Rose. There is something else that bothers him but I cannot tell you," Catherine looked extremely uncomfortable. "It's not an easy matter to speak of."

It suddenly dawned on Rose why Patrick had grown so irritable.

"Have you not permitted him to lie with you?" she asked.

"Do we not share the same bed? What manner of question is that?" Catherine was more embarrassed than annoyed.

"Do not play me for a fool, young lady. You know exactly what I'm speaking of," Rose's voice was unusually harsh.

Catherine shook her head, hiding her face behind the flannel.

"How are you to explain the birth of a baby if you do not give yourself to your husband?" Rose was trying to be sensitive but her question caused a fresh flood of tears.

"I cannot. As soon as Patrick lays a hand on me I shrink away from him. He has been as patient as a saint but I fear I will never be able to give him what he needs. I shall take the boat home to my parents. They will assume the child is Patrick's."

"Do you care for him at all, Catherine?" asked Rose.

"I do, very much so. But I will never be a wife to him. It was wrong of me to deceive him."

"You are not the first bride to have this problem. Even if he is angry with you, take his hand in yours tonight and beg him to be patient a little longer. I know he will, he's a good man, Catherine, and you must trust that he will never hurt you," Rose gently cupped her niece's face between her hands, forcing eye contact. "If he finds out that he has been tricked into rearing another man's child, he may never forgive you. Think on that, my love. Time is running out for you."

Owen had a scowl on his face when Rose joined him in the parlour. She asked if he would search for Patrick and bring him back. Then she decided to confide in him what had been bothering the young man, but did not tell him of Catherine's pregnancy.

"Well, that explains a lot, doesn't it now?" he said. "I know exactly where to look for him. The nearest alehouse. I'll be off so. Don't wait up for us, Rose, it would be best if he didn't have to face you when we return."

"Be kind to him, Owen, and none of your usual jesting, do you hear? His father is still warm in the grave. Had he been alive, I'm sure Patrick would have turned to him for counsel."

Raucous, male laughter met Owen at the first public house he came to and he was not surprised to find Patrick inside. He knew by the look on the young man's face that he was already intoxicated.

"What are you, the messenger boy?" Patrick slurred when Owen spoke quietly in his ear. "Well you can go back and tell my good wife that I'm with people who like my company. Is that not so, boys?"

Two young men a few years older than Patrick, sat either side of him and raised their drinks in salute. Draining their tankards before slamming them onto the counter top, they put their arms around him and helped him to his feet.

"Come with us Patrick, we're off down the docks to find ourselves a bit of female company," one of them said.

"Maybe I should, maybe I should," muttered Patrick.

Owen stepped forward and pulled him from between the men, "It seems I got here in the nick of time. Let's be getting you home, lad."

Patrick allowed himself to be led outside, staggering as soon as the cooler air hit him. He offered no resistance as Owen took hold of his wrist and pulled a limp arm across a pair of broad shoulders. However, he refused to answer any questions put to him.

The house was quiet when they stepped through the door, as Rose had gone to bed early and Catherine had fallen asleep in her room, emotionally drained and exhausted from weeping.

"Get this down you. You smell like a brewery, son," Owen placed some tea on the table and sat opposite Patrick.

"I know what your problem is, lad. Getting drunk will only make it worse. You may be tempted to do something you'll regret."

"I don't have a problem. I have a wife that has a problem," Patrick spoke in an even tone.

"That may well be the case, but you're a married man now and any problem your wife has becomes yours, too," said Owen. "Give her time. The poor girl is worn out from long hours at the laundry, that's not the sort of work she has been accustomed to. And that letter she received from her father was enough to take the wind out of anyone's sails. Mind you, I cannot blame him for what he said,"

Owen refilled Patrick's empty cup. "I would not like to be in your shoes when you next lay eyes on my brother."

CHAPTER TWENTY-SIX

As Rose lifted the eggs from the hot water she heard footsteps on the stairs and assumed it was Catherine.

"I have some breakfast made. Call the men, love, while it's still hot."

"It's me, Rose. Catherine is not feeling well this morning, she won't be coming to Mass with us," Patrick sniffed the air. "It's the smell of the bacon that has me up and dressed in such haste."

"You sound very jolly for a change, young man."

Rose turned from the stove and almost dropped the plate of poached eggs. Patrick had the biggest smile plastered across his face.

"Why wouldn't I be? Sure isn't this a grand start to a fine day?" he sniffed the air as he beamed.

Rose looked at the rain spitting against the window, but made no remark on the weather.

"Good food, a warm home," Patrick continued and pointed to Owen, who had just come down the stairs. "And pleasant company to boot. What more could a man ask for?"

Owen raised an eyebrow at his wife and Rose made an excuse to leave the parlour, for fear she would laugh out loud.

"I think Catherine might be able to manage an egg this morning," she said, carrying a plate towards the stairs.

"But she never eats in the morning, Rose. I'll bring her up a cup of tea," offered Patrick.

"I think she might manage a poached egg. You two get on with your meal. Tell Patrick the news you gave me last night, Owen, while I bring this up to Catherine."

Leaving her puzzled husband to share an imaginary story, she climbed the stairs to her niece's room and knocked on the door before opening it.

"Wait a few weeks before throwing up in front of your husband, Catherine. He might think it's a wee bit early for pregnancy sickness."

"Oh Rose, how did you guess, surely he didn't tell you," Catherine was mortified.

"He didn't have to. He's downstairs wearing the most foolish grin I've ever seen on a man's face. I couldn't sit at the table and look at it," laughed Rose.

"I can't eat the egg, but the tea is good, thank you," Catherine took a sip of the hot liquid.

"I'm sorry to go on about Patrick like that. It was thoughtless of me. Is there anything you would like to ask me, or tell me?" asked Rose.

Catherine shook her head, "I would rather not speak of such things, if you don't mind."

"Right, my love, I'll leave you be. If you fancy the egg later it will be on the back of the stove. We'll be off soon and you'll have the house to yourself."

Later that morning, Owen and Rose could not take their eyes off Patrick as he laughed and joked outside the church. They stood waiting for him while he chatted with a workmate and his wife.

"I take it there will be no more need to drag him from an alehouse," Owen whispered and smiled knowingly at his wife.

"I truly hope so. I'm worn out from the misery that moved into our house with that young couple," said Rose.

As the weeks went by, things did get better between the newlyweds. Catherine's bouts of sickness disappeared and her work at the laundry became more bearable. Patrick raced home after a long day at the quarry to spend every minute he could with his young wife. He soon won over her trust with his gentle manner and affectionate nature.

One sunny December morning Patrick woke to find the space beside him empty and a distinct aroma of bacon drifting into the room. He quickly dressed and headed downstairs to the parlour.

Catherine was standing by the stove, having made breakfast for the household, when she felt Patrick's arms encircle her waist. He waited for her body to go rigid, her usual reaction to even the lightest touch of his hand. Instead, she leaned back into him and turned her head to kiss his unshaven cheek.

"I can't make up my mind which smells better, you or the bacon," Patrick sniffed and kissed the side of her neck.

"What a cheek, why me, of course. It's that lavender soap you gave me yesterday, for our three month anniversary."

"And is this fine breakfast your present to me?" he asked.

"No, I wanted to save Rose the bother of rising so early for a change. I told her last night that I would take a turn with breakfast this morning."

Catherine placed the food on the table.

"But I do have a present for you, of sorts. I'll tell you about it now, before I call the others," she sat on a chair next to her husband and took his hand in hers. "I am with child, Patrick. I hope you'll not be too dismayed that it has happened so quickly."

Bringing his palm to her abdomen she asked if he had noticed that it was swollen.

"I had indeed noticed, but your appetite has improved of late. I thought it might be that."

Patrick left his hand where she had placed it and felt a sense of wonder at the prospect of being a father. He was surprised that not even one anxious thought had entered his head.

"So if I were to grow fat as I get older, you will still care for me?" laughed Catherine.

"Of course, and if am to lose my hair, as my father did, I expect you to feel the same way about me."

"We have a deal," said Catherine and offered her hand.

It was the welcome sight of a young couple laughing and shaking hands that met Owen and Rose as they entered the parlour.

Patrick stood behind his wife and placed both hands on her shoulders.

"He has that foolish grin on his face again," Owen whispered in Rose's ear.

"Catherine and I have some good news for you," said Patrick.

"You're moving out, at last. We'll have a party," joked Owen.

Rose dug her husband in the ribs, full sure that she knew what the young man was about to say, "Stop your teasing, Owen. Don't mind this great big oaf, tell us your news, lad."

"Catherine and myself are to become parents in . . ." Patrick turned to his wife, "How many months?"

The young woman quickly calculated the months and added two more. Rose held her breath, afraid that her niece might not think before answering.

"I would say . . . perhaps . . . six months from now. That would take us to sometime in May. Yes, I'm sure it will be in May," Catherine beamed at her aunt.

"It might even be sooner than that. Babies have a habit of surprising us with their hurry to get into the world," said Rose.

"That's very true, our twins, God rest their little souls, came a full month before their time, if I remember correctly. Is that not so, Rose?" asked Owen.

"Why yes it is. In fact, I think they may have come almost two months earlier than expected. That was why they were such sickly children."

When Rose saw the look of concern on Patrick's face she quickly added, "But I was carrying two babies, at a time when we had very little food. I'm sure Catherine's wee one will be hale and hearty."

"I feel very well indeed and not a trace of sickness. In fact I'm so hungry I could eat every scrap on this table," Catherine smiled at her aunt.

She made a mental note to thank her for bringing up the fact that some babies are born prematurely. Patrick would need to be reminded of that when the time arrived.

CHAPTER TWENTY-SEVEN

James tapped both chisels further into the rock until an almost straight line appeared across the breadth of it.

"This is the last one we'll do for today. We're losing the light," he said.

"I won't argue with that," said Matthew Clark, easing the newly split rock apart, "I have never met a man to build a wall as quickly as yourself, James."

"When I'm being paid on what I have quoted for the work and not for how many days I labour, it helps to speed things up. I learned what I know from Mary's father, rest his soul. The poor man lies somewhere in Leitrim. That's the last place we were able to track him to."

"Those were hard times, James. Hard times indeed. Who knows how many starving souls dropped dead in the fields and ditches of Ireland? Mary has relatives in America, does she not?" asked Matthew.

"They were very young when they settled there, once a year a letter arrives and we reply with our own bit of news. What of your son Daniel? How is he faring over there, is he still working on the docks?"

"He has recently moved away from the city, it was never to his liking, especially now that he has a family to rear. He's in a place called Montana, where a lot of Irish have settled, and he has taken a lease on a farm," said Matthew.

"They say there's opportunity there if you have a mind to grasp it. Young Daniel might yet have his own piece of land. At least he's safe enough, unlike his friend, John McDermott," James lowered his voice and looked around, in spite of them being alone. "Are you not relieved that your son is too preoccupied feeding his family to accompany young John and his fellow Fenians on their invasions of Canada?"

Matthew shook his head sadly, "Any attempt of that sort is doomed to failure. All they have accomplished is a split in the Brotherhood, just as sure as you've cut that stone in half."

"They have thousands of well-trained Irish soldiers that fought on both sides of the civil war over there," replied James. "You cannot blame them for thinking they have a chance at using the attack on Canadian soil to keep the Crown busy, while they gain a foothold here."

"We are not yet ready for a rising in Ireland. There have been too many failures in the past because of divided opinion and ill timing," Matthew replied.

James cleaned and wrapped up his chisels in their cloth bag, noting that he would need to pay a visit to the blacksmith to have them sharpened.

"We might not have solved the problem of Ireland's fight for freedom, Matthew, but we have built a fine wall that will still be here for our grandchildren to sit on. Let's pray they will be citizens of their own country by then, for I cannot see that it will come about in our lifetime."

It was quite late as James drove his cart past Paddy Mac's, having first dropped

Matthew Clarke home. He could see a group of men standing by the door and knew instinctively that a clandestine meeting was taking place. Even if he had wanted to become an active member of the local Fenian circle, he would not have been welcome.

It was well known how much attention District Inspector Armstrong paid to James McGrother and it was not something the Brotherhood invited. On occasion, it had been used to their advantage and James had willingly allowed that, as long as his family were in no danger of suffering any form of reprisal.

Having settled the donkey his children had named Rí into the outhouse for the night, James sniffed the salty air and relished the thought of the following night's fishing out in the bay. The cottage was unusually quiet when he stepped inside and Mary was sitting by the fire, mending clothes.

"Have the children gone to bed already? Are they not well?"

"Here is your supper, James," Mary placed a bowl on the table, next to a platter of potatoes. "I have some news for you and I did not wish for the children to hear it. They are staying with Maggie tonight and will call here in the morning before setting out for school."

James felt the old familiar pounding in his chest at the seriousness of her tone. He began to eat his meal but the hunger had left him and he picked at his food in the silence that hung between them.

"Well, tell me the bad news, Mary. I can see by your face something unpleasant is about to befall us."

Mary smiled weakly and sighed, "No, James. The news would be very pleasant indeed, if I were giving it to anyone else but you. Maggie received word from Catherine that she is with child. Is it not a sad state of affairs when our own married daughter is in fear of telling us her good news?"

James banged the table with his fist and was about to give vent to his rage when Mary cut him short.

"That is exactly why I made sure the children were not here whilst I spoke to you on this matter. Will you now confide in me – your wife – as to the reason you withheld your blessing on their marriage? Patrick Gallagher is a good man and we could not have chosen a better husband for our daughter."

The look of sadness and confusion on his wife's face deflated James and he slumped against the back of his chair. His family had given them a present of a mantle clock when they left England earlier in the year. The sound of it's ticking in the quietness of the house reminded James of a similar situation he had been in with his brother Owen. On that occasion, a long held secret had been shared and no harm had come about because of it.

"Patrick may have killed a man," James blurted it out.

"What nonsense is that? Who told you so, Patrick himself? Otherwise, I will not believe it

137

to be true," Mary was shocked but remained calm.

"Before he died, I received a letter from his father. It was a blessing that both of us could read and write, as the information it contained was best kept between ourselves. Thomas Gallagher did not even risk posting it in an envelope, but sent it in a package. Do you recall that parcel of newspapers I received from him, about seven months back? Well, inside was the news that I feared was true."

James went on to tell Mary the real reason behind the young man's visit to Blackrock.

"So his lungs were not as weak as he made out. Instead he bore a knife wound in his side," said Mary. "I'm sure Catherine has noticed *that* by now. I wonder what excuse he gave her. Bitten by a shark no doubt, or some such nonsense, to impress the lovesick daughter of a fisherman."

"Now do you see why I could not give them my blessing? I tried my best to put Catherine off. For a while, it seemed that she had listened to my counsel. Somehow he managed to talk her around."

"What did his father say in the letter? Do you still have it?" asked Mary.

"You know better than to ask me that. The letter was thrown into the fire the minute I read it. Thomas Gallagher insisted that his son is unsure about the events and that he was not one to use a knife in a brawl. Two men approached him as he walked home from work one evening. They had been with his son at the time of the assault and witnessed the struggle between Patrick and his assailant. It seems that after receiving the stab wound to his side, our young son-by-marriage fought back even harder and by the time his friends reached him, the other man lay spread out on top of him. When they pulled him off Patrick, the man's own knife was thrust deep into his chest."

James paused as Mary's hands flew to her mouth.

"Thomas Gallagher apologized for taking advantage of his friendship with my family, but he said it was the only way he could get his son out of the country at the time. He feared that Patrick would die on the journey over, and wrote that he was eternally grateful for the care Maggie and Kitty gave him."

"It was an accident so. Sure the lad was only trying to defend himself. Have the police been looking for him?" asked Mary.

"The men involved on both sides are most likely sworn to secrecy. They will all be accused of wrongdoing no matter what side they are on. I doubt that any of them are willing to spend time in prison. But that does not mean Patrick is in the clear. These things have a way of hanging over a man's head, Mary."

"Please, James, pay more heed to your choice of words. *Hanging* is not one that should be included in this conversation," Mary scolded.

Once the tension between them had eased, James could see how upsetting the news had been for his wife. She only ever chewed a fingernail when she was seriously bothered by something and he noted that Mary was now on her third nail. He knew that she needed to be distracted from the same train of thought that had caused himself so much anxiety.

"In all our fussing over young Patrick and his unfortunate encounter, we have forgotten one important thing, love."

"And what would that be, James?" asked Mary, still chewing.

"We have a new grandchild on the way. Does that not cheer you up a wee bit?"

"Oh, merciful heaven, it certainly does. What on earth are we fretting over? Something that may never come to pass. Like that buffoon Armstrong, wasting his time trying to catch you up to no good. If only he would hold his breath while he waits. That would get rid of him good and proper," laughed Mary.

CHAPTER TWENTY-EIGHT

Catherine's aunt stood to one side and watched anxiously as the midwife ran her hands methodically across her swollen belly.

"Is it as I suspect?" Rose asked.

The woman nodded, "At this late stage I doubt the baby will turn and it's not a small one at that. Will you not listen to your aunt and let the doctor try to turn the poor wee mite?"

Catherine vehemently refused to go anywhere near the hospital, "He was my employer, it would be too embarrassing. No, I trust yourself and Rose to look after me. Surely you have birthed a baby feet first before?" she asked.

"I have, and lost a few. It's very dangerous for the child. If it is still breech when your time comes, you had best take advantage of Doctor Henshaw's experience in these matters," the midwife advised. "He is the only doctor I would trust to deliver a baby, Catherine. Rose see if you can talk some sense into your niece."

After the midwife had gone the two women were unusually quiet as they prepared the evening meal. Patrick had insisted that Catherine give up her work at the laundry. Although the recent wet weather had meant less work for the quarrymen, Patrick always found an odd job here or there for the slack days.

"I fear you are very near your time, girl, and I'm sure Mrs. Cooper suspects the same," Rose smiled at her niece's worried expression.

"There's no need to fret, she is very discreet in matters of that nature. Your secret is safe with her."

A week later found Catherine in labour and Mrs. Cooper advising Patrick to take his wife immediately to the hospital.

"A baby does not have much chance of survival being born so early," she said, but in truth it was the breech delivery of a fine sized child that concerned her more. The midwife had her suspicions about the due date of Patrick's young wife but never aired them.

A carriage arrived outside their door and a very irate young woman was carried to it by her husband.

"Please, love, stop with your shrieking, unless it's the pain that's causing it. I'll not risk any harm to you or our child for the sake of superstitious nonsense," he said.

Patrick climbed in beside his wife and Rose sat in front of them. She had sent a message to Doctor Henshaw's residence a couple of hours earlier, and prayed for Catherine's sake he would already be at the hospital waiting for them.

"It was very good of him to offer his assistance should any problems arise with your labour, Catherine. He is the best doctor in the north of England," Rose tried to assure her niece.

"There is far more risk of death when a woman gives birth in a hospital. I've heard it said that they succumb to a fever. Please listen to me, Patrick, for it is not a superstition. Tell him Rose. Please I beg of you, turn the carriage back now – owww," a band of pain tightened across Catherine's abdomen, cutting short her pleading.

"I will be with you right through the birth," said Rose. "You are beginning to tire out. This past twenty hours of your labour has drained you of your strength, Catherine."

"Then I will have the baby here, in this carriage, this very minute," the young woman began to push in desperation.

"Stop behaving so selfishly, Catherine. You will do neither yourself nor your baby any good," snapped Rose.

As soon as the carriage came to a halt, Patrick jumped down and carried his struggling wife through the doors of the hospital. Rose was relieved to find Doctor Henshaw already there waiting for their arrival.

In spite of her exhaustion and painful contractions, Catherine persistently demanded to be brought home and placed under the care of an experienced midwife. She was past caring whether or not she insulted her former employer.

"My dear girl, if your baby is breech and coming so soon before it's time, then the safest place for both of you is here. I qualified as a doctor in Scotland, where midwifery is part of the training. So I assure you, Catherine, I know what I'm doing and I have a very good record for the safe delivery of babies and the survival of their mothers."

Patrick was asked to remain in the waiting area while Catherine was rushed away, Rose accompanying her. As she was being helped onto a bed, she grabbed her aunt by the skirt and pulled her close.

"What is it, love? Don't be afraid, I won't leave you."

"Please, Rose, send Patrick home. I don't trust myself as to what I might say. It would be best if he were not here when the baby comes. Tell him the doctor said to come back in the morning."

Rose agreed that Patrick should be sent home. Doctor Henshaw would know that Catherine's baby was full term and Rose would need to have a quiet word with him about not mentioning that fact to the young man.

A few seconds after her aunt had left the room a very strong contraction forced Catherine to push. Her vision blurred as the pain consumed her and she became aware of male voices speaking, one of them urging her to stop pushing. Upon opening her eyes the young woman was confronted with a scene that caused her to scramble backwards, away from the end of the bed.

"Catherine please compose yourself. Do you remember Doctor Gilmore? I am teaching him the skills of midwifery. Surely you are grateful to have the assistance of two doctors?" said Doctor Henshaw.

"No. I want nothing from *him*. Rose, ROSE," screamed Catherine.

Gilmore glanced at his colleague and placed a few drops of chloroform on a piece of cloth. Holding it over her nose and mouth, he lowered his head until his lips were close to

Catherine's ear, and pretended to speak soothingly to the distressed young woman.

"You had better cooperate if you know what's good for you, my dear," his whisper was harsh and vindictive.

"Just enough to calm her down but not render her unconscious, Doctor Gilmore," said Henshaw, running his hands around the shape of a bulging womb. "Your baby is well on the way, Catherine. You must do exactly as I tell you and no harm will come to either of you. Are you paying heed to me, my dear?"

"Yes, I'm listening, Doctor Henshaw" whispered Catherine, "Please send for my aunt. She will help me follow your instructions."

At that moment, Rose came through the door and kissed her niece's forehead before laying a cold compress upon it. Placing her hand in Catherine's, she told her to squeeze it with all her might on the next wave of pain.

After twenty minutes of pushing, then holding, then pushing again, according to the commands of Doctor Henshaw, a fine sized baby boy was safely delivered, feet first. Once he was satisfied that both of his patients were in good health, Doctor Henshaw left the room with his colleague in tow.

Rose made sure that Catherine and the baby were clean and comfortable and gave her niece some advice about nursing a new-born infant. He instinctively knew how to latch onto her breast and immediately began to suckle.

"Well, that one's been here before. Would you look at him feed? No doubt he'll walk early

145

too. You'll have your hands full with him, girl, mark my words," laughed Rose.

Catherine could not take her eyes from the head of black hair that felt soft and silky against her arm. As she fussed about the bed, Rose noticed teardrops landing on the baby's face.

"Are you in pain, Catherine?" she asked.

"A wee bit, but it's nothing that I cannot bear."

Pulling a chair closer to the bed, Rose sat down and swept a lock of Catherine's hair behind her ear. She was troubled to see tears streaming down the pretty, young face.

"At times I wished him dead. Can you believe that? A mother having such terrible thoughts about her own child. It's not his fault, the way he came to be made, poor wee mite. When we discovered he was breech, I thought that God had answered my prayers, but I didn't want any harm to come to him by then. Now I have him in my arms, I would kill anyone who tried to harm him," Catherine looked at her aunt. "I'm very grateful to Doctor Henshaw for his help, will you tell him that Rose? And apologize for my behaviour."

"Do you want me to fetch Patrick? He'll be on edge waiting for the news. I'll come back with him, I promise. Doctor Henshaw will give him leave to visit you, if I ask."

Catherine grabbed her aunt's wrist, digging her nails into the flesh, "Please don't leave me here alone, or I'll take my baby and run after you the moment you are gone."

The desperation in her voice was enough to tell Rose that she meant every word of what was said.

"Hush now, girl. I won't go till you say so. How about a nice cup of tea? I could certainly do with one myself. I'll hurry back."

Five minutes after Rose had left the room Catherine was swapping her baby from one breast to the other, when the door slowly opened.

"That's the quickest cup of tea I've ever seen made," she laughed, her eyes glued to her child.

"So, my dear, we have a son."

The bile rose in Catherine's throat as Doctor Gilmore's contemptuous voice reached her ears. She clutched her baby even closer to her breast and pulled a shawl around him, concealing herself and her child from his lewd gaze.

"If you take one more step nearer I will scream with all my might."

"I doubt that very much, Catherine. I seem to remember you were not so quick to scream on the night our son was conceived," Gilmore moved towards the bed. "That is not a premature baby you hold to your breast. I wager that husband of yours has had the wool pulled over his eyes regarding the lineage of his new son. Am I correct in saying so?"

"Correct in what, may I ask, Doctor Gilmore?" Rose had just come through the door carrying a tray.

"Oh, I was just guessing what name your niece will give to her young son. He will no doubt be named after his paternal

147

grandfather, is that not the tradition?" Gilmore gave Catherine a devious smile.

Rose noted the strange look that passed between them, and knew instantly what had caused Catherine's face to drain of colour and beads of sweat to form on her brow. The young woman's emphatic refusal to go to the hospital was beginning to make sense to her aunt.

Gilmore turned on his heel without waiting for a response and left the room as quietly as he had entered.

"You don't have to say a word, a nod of the head will do. Was he the man that assaulted you, my love?" Rose whispered.

Catherine nodded her head, never taking her eyes from the door.

"Oh my poor child. No wonder you couldn't tell me the truth. Nobody will take your word against a man of his standing. We must never tell anyone else about this. If Patrick or your father were to find out, Gilmore's fancy pedigree would not protect him from their wrath. They would both swing for what they would do to him."

It took another thirty minutes before Catherine fell into an exhausted sleep. Her energy was spent from two days of labour, a difficult breech delivery and the stress of coming face to face with Gilmore once again.

Rose checked that both mother and baby were in a deep sleep before leaving the room. She located a young trainee nurse and warned her to stay by Catherine's bed until her return.

On passing the door to Doctor Henshaw's office she heard his voice ring out.

"Rose, is that you? Could you come in for a moment, please?"

"Yes Doctor Henshaw, is there something I can do for you?"

"Is your niece comfortable? I was quite taken aback at her hysterics."

"Oh yes, thank you doctor. Catherine is in good form and much calmer now," said Rose.

"Good, good. However I am still concerned. Her behaviour was highly unusual. I have made some notes but I fear there was something other than childbirth that gave rise to her distress. I take it you realize that the child is not premature, Rose, but you can count on my discretion. I see now why the poor girl was in such haste to marry. What manner of man is her husband? Does Catherine have a morbid fear of him?"

Rose was lost for words as to how she should respond to such questions. To make matters worse, Doctor Gilmore had come through the door behind her. He stood so close, her flesh crawled at the light touch of his breath upon her neck.

"Catherine's husband is one of the finest young men you could ever encounter," Rose took a step forward. "She has not had one unhappy day since they wed. I would put her hysteria down to her great fear of childbirth, nothing more, Doctor Henshaw. In fact Catherine asked me to apologize for her outburst and to thank you for the safe delivery of her baby. Would you like me to fetch you some tea?"

"That's very good of you to offer, Mrs. McGrother, but I have just arranged for a tray to be sent here to the office," said Gilmore.

Doctor Henshaw seemed satisfied with Rose's explanation for her niece's erratic behaviour and instructed her to continue on with her business. As she neared the kitchens Rose met one of the nurses carrying a tea tray.

"Is that for Doctor Gilmore," she asked, taking it from her.

"And for Doctor Henshaw. It's to go to his office."

"I'll take it, I must convey a message to him. Might as well save you the journey," said Rose.

When she returned to the doctor's office the two men were deep in conversation and barely looked at her as she entered the room. Standing with her back to them, Rose bent her head over one of the cups. Into it she dropped a large glob of phlegm and spittle she had been gathering at the back of her throat, on her way up the corridor.

"Milk and sugar, Doctor Gilmore?" she asked.

"Oh, it's you again. I thought you had left for home," he sneered.

"On no, sir. I'm here, there, everywhere, keeping a watchful eye on things. Did you say both?" asked Rose.

"Both?" Gilmore was confused by her words.

"Milk and sugar."

Having been told his preference, Rose handed the cup of well stirred tea sugar and phlegm, to the man whose life she intended to make as miserable as possible.

"Rose makes a proper cup of tea, don't you, my dear?" quipped Henshaw.

She gave them a big smile and a tiny curtsy, before leaving the room. In the corridor Rose paused long enough to see Gilmore take a long drink from his cup, before hurrying to the exit to hail a carriage for home.

Owen would have berated her if she had walked at such a late hour by herself and would be more than willing to pay her fare. Rose leaned back into the velvet cushioned seat, smiling to herself at such luxury and twice in one day at that. Then the image of Gilmore unknowingly drinking her spittle came to mind and she laughed so hard, her sides hurt and tears ran down her face.

CHAPTER TWENTY-NINE

It was not unusual for Michael Kiernan to keep a low profile. The man who had acted as a decoy, using Michael's American papers, had played his part well in leaving a trail across the width of that vast continent. He had been quite happy with Michael's proposal and although the general labouring he found along the way was difficult, the adventure on foreign soil made up for it.

James had even received a letter from America, supposedly from his friend Michael, thanking him for organizing his son's funeral. Even Brigid, his estranged wife, was under the impression that he was off to New Orleans or some such place. She didn't really care where his travels took him, as long as it was far enough away from herself and their children.

With the introduction of steamships the journey across the Atlantic had been greatly reduced, much to Brigid's relief. She was anxious to see her family after so many years.

A few days were spent with her mother, who was no longer a domestic in one of the big houses of Liverpool, but lived instead with her youngest daughter and son-in-law. It was a reunion of mixed emotions after two decades apart, as the main reason for the trip played on everyone's minds.

Brigid's son, Francis, had stayed with his aunt's family and spent many hours becoming acquainted with his grandmother and cousins before continuing his ill-fated journey to Ireland. The fact that his mother was on her way to his grave, dampened what should have been a joyous occasion.

Unaware of his wife's impending visit to Blackrock, Michael was making his way there in the hopes of enlisting the aid of a man he knew he could trust. It had been extremely difficult avoiding recognition, which was why Michael had moved from county to county, only staying in the larger towns where he could keep a low profile. He had grown a beard and wore the clothes of a wandering labourer.

Small towns and villages were not the best places to remain anonymous, as strangers stuck out like sore thumbs and would only attract attention. As Michael's journey brought him nearer to his home county of Louth, he took to sleeping in barns and outhouses and avoided traveling by road. Traversing the fields by daylight from Ardee to Dromiskin, Michael waited until the evening had drawn in before crossing the boundary of his native parish.

Under cover of darkness, a tired and hungry Michael Kiernan finally arrived at his destination, satisfied that he had not left a trail behind him. It was of the upmost importance that everyone acquainted with him believed him to be in America – regardless of whether they were friend or foe.

Having watched the house for almost an hour, Matthew sank back further into the bushes when he saw the door open and a tall man step outside. His frame was outlined by a beam of light pouring into the blackness that surrounded the cottage.

Michael was thankful for the cover of a cloudy night as he gave a signal to alert the man of his presence. It only took Matthew Clarke five seconds to reach the place where the sound had come from.

"Who goes there?"

"It's Michael Kiernan."

The dark shape moved closer and thrust out a hand. The two men embraced and Matthew led his visitor to a lean-to at the back of his house.

"Michael, have you just arrived from America? Do you need a place to stay?"

Having explained that another man was using his papers in America, Michael assured Matthew that he was the only one who knew of his whereabouts.

"I suppose you've come to meet up with your wife," said Matthew.

"My wife? Is Brigid here?"

"Not yet, but I hear she is due to arrive soon. She's visiting her family in Liverpool. Where you unaware of her plans? You sound surprised."

There wasn't a word from Michael and after a few moments Matthew spoke again.

"So, you are here for a different reason. What might that be, or are you under an oath of secrecy?"

"I beg your pardon, Matthew, but I cannot disclose my reason for being here. Suffice it to say I did not expect to hear that my wife was on her way. I thought she was in America."

"I'm sure she thinks the same about yourself, Michael, as we have all been led to believe."

"No one must know that I'm in Ireland. Swear an oath not to tell anyone, Matthew. Not even James McGrother can be told. If word gets out then my mission will be sure to fail."

"You have my word that I will tell no one. What is it you need from me? A place to stay?"

"I need ammunition. I have a pistol but nothing to put into it. I lost my bag crossing a river. In fact, I nearly lost all my clothes too. They were in a bundle on my head and I stumbled on a rock."

Matthew gave a quiet laugh, "Now that would be a sorry sight, you standing on the bank of a river stark naked, wearing nothing but a frown."

"Aye, it would indeed. My white rump would not have been too easily hidden among the foliage."

"Wait here. I must let my wife know I'll be away for a wee while," Matthew disappeared into the blackness.

Michael watched as the dark shape ran back towards the cottage. He thought about his own wife and how sad she must be at the task ahead of her, for he knew instinctively what that was. Brigid would be on her way to pray at her son's grave before she could put him to rest. With all his heart, Michael yearned to hold her once more, so they might console one another, but he knew it was not to be.

"Michael, follow me."

Matthew Clarke's voice broke into his thoughts. When they came to a low stone wall bordering a field, he took out a length of cloth.

"I'm sorry Michael but I must blindfold you."

"I understand. I would do the same to you. I pray you won't be guiding me through any streams, now that you are aware of my clumsy footing."

An hour later, Michael Kiernan was bidding farewell to his friend, before racing through the night to a fate he could no longer avoid.

CHAPTER THIRTY

As Catherine slowly woke up from a deep slumber she was aware of a man's low murmuring voice next to her bed. Happy in the knowledge that Patrick was beside her, she smiled and kept her eyes tightly shut. She decided to tease him by pretending to be asleep, and turned onto her side with her back to him.

"He's a handsome boy, my dear. We make excellent babies together, do you not think so?"

The young mother froze as her eyes shot open. The thought of such a man touching her child sent a shiver of revulsion through her body and she turned towards the voice, sitting up as she did.

"He has nothing to do with you, I married his father. We had a moment of weakness and as soon as Patrick found out I was with child he did the decent thing. I would not expect you to understand decency, knowing what you are capable of. Now, give me my son and kindly leave the room."

A look of shock crossed the doctor's face at Catherine's words. He had taken her for a mouse of a girl, with no backbone. This was a pleasant surprise, making her even more attractive to him than she already was.

Just as he was about to answer, he heard someone step into the room behind him and a smile lit up the young mother's face.

"I'm sorry doctor, I'll go back into the corridor until you have finished examining the baby," Patrick apologized.

"NO," Catherine shouted, making the baby jump. "Doctor Gilmore was about to leave, is that not so?" she looked at the man beside her bed with newly found courage.

"Please give my son to his father, Doctor."

Catherine watched as the baby was passed between the two men. She noted how grim the doctor's face had become and prayed that her young husband would not see it himself. However, she needn't have worried as Patrick was so taken with the child in his arms, he had eyes for no one else, not even his wife.

"He has the look of my father and my brother Tom. Do you not think so, Catherine?"

"That was exactly what I thought the moment I laid eyes on him, with his head of black hair," Catherine looked defiantly at the doctor and saw a flash of anger cross his face.

"Well, I'll give you both some privacy, excuse me," Gilmore nodded stiffly and left the room.

"I can leave with you this evening, Patrick. Doctor Henshaw is happy enough to release me into the care of my aunt for my lying-in. He says I'm as fit as a fiddle and will no doubt have a dozen more healthy babies," laughed Catherine.

"Well now, I wasn't exactly planning on that many. Do you want me to call Rose? She's talking to one of the nurses in the hallway."

Please do, Patrick. I'll be dressed in no time at all. I cannot wait to bring wee Thomas home to meet the rest of the family."

Although Catherine's baby was supposed to have been born about four weeks early nobody questioned the fact that he was a fine sized child. There was the odd remark that it was a lucky thing for his mother, for if he had grown any bigger he would have been well and truly stuck.

"Are you pleased with your son?" Catherine asked as she nursed him, enjoying her first night back in her own bed.

Patrick was lying alongside her stroking the baby's head, happy to have them both home safe and sound.

"More than pleased, love, proud as punch. I have to confess, I'm also a wee bit afraid of him. How do you know what ails a baby when he is crying?"

"You don't always know for sure, but if there's no fever or coughing and he is still feeding, then it can't be too serious. Babies cry to be picked up, too. We must be careful not to spoil him, Patrick, although I fear you have already fallen into that trap. As soon as he hears your voice he wails."

"That's what worries me. I was thinking he didn't like me," said Patrick.

"He's a clever wee mite. He's only been with you on four occasions and yet he knows you will take him in your arms if he cries out. Your son loves you already, Patrick."

******

Mary sighed contentedly having listened to her husband read two letters to her, one after the other.

"Who would believe we received news from both children on the same day, and them in two different countries at that?" she said.

159

"Unusual, I would say," James turned the envelopes over scrutinizing them. "I hope they haven't been tampered with. Matthew Clarke is convinced his son's letters are opened before he receives them."

"That's foolish talk, James. It would take an army of spies to look at every letter coming into the country. Sure there isn't that many people who can read in Ireland," Mary laughed.

"I suppose you're right. Well now, what do you think about your new grandchild, and a boy at that?"

"I hope your pleasant tone means you have forgiven Patrick for marrying our Catherine."

"It's too late now to change anything, unless I were to kill him with my bare hands for sneaking off behind my back and courting her."

"Make a widow of your own daughter, would you James McGrother?" Mary teased.

"You know I'm not one to bear grudges, love. I shall give young Patrick a stern look for all of ten seconds and then put him out of his misery. Is that agreeable to you?" James lied for the sake of peace.

"It is indeed, and I shall enjoy his ten seconds of gloom as much as yourself. It's a fair punishment, James. He deserves that much at least."

Although the letter from Catherine caused the most excitement, it was his son's correspondence that held James's attention. He was still thinking about it long after they had gone to bed.

160

Thomas's letter answered many questions that James had wanted to ask Michael on the few occasions they had met or corresponded over the years. He had always wondered why his friend, who had left England full of the hope of acquiring his own piece of land, had never fulfilled that dream. James knew that they would have needed to work in New York for the first few years after their arrival, but Michael and Brigid's plan had been to homestead eventually.

With sleep escaping him, James dragged himself out of his bed. Unlike his head, his body wanted to lie still and rest. He pulled over the curtain that was draped around the bed, so as not to disturb Mary when he lit a candle. The letter from his son had been placed in a tin box next to a tea caddy – the two most important containers in the house. Both held papers of high value to James and Mary, precious letters from family in one, and hard earned money in the other.

Both tins were stored behind a lose stone to the side of the fireplace and as James took the box of letters out, the scrape of metal on rock echoed in the quietness of the parlour. Holding his breath he looked towards the bed, regretting fumbling about in the dark and not lighting a candle beforehand.

There wasn't a stir from behind the drapes so James poked a thin piece of kindling into the hot ash and lit the wick. With the shadow of a flame dancing on the ceiling, he sat by the fireside and squinted at the words Thomas had written. As usual, the second James laid eyes on the neat script, a wave of longing swept over him for his eldest son.

The letter told him of the young man's travels in his work as a reporter. Thomas's description of the fate of his fellow countrymen, upon arrival in their new land, gave James an insight as to what had become of Michael and Brigid's dream.

Most of the Irish, fleeing from extreme poverty and starvation during the famine years, had the immediate task of finding employment upon arrival. Those fortunate enough often found work through family and friends from home, who were already well settled. As time went by, the younger children attended school and families regularly congregated at their church, becoming part of a securely tight knit, if overcrowded, community.

James could see why Brigid would be hesitant to stray further afield and venture into a vast, unknown landscape. If it had been just the two of them, he was sure the young couple would have moved on in search of land, but they had a young child to think of.

"Oh, Michael, if only you had followed your dream. What is to become of you now?" James whispered.

Mary's hands resting on his shoulders startled him and both of them apologized to the other at the same time.

"Ah sure, I wasn't having a pleasant sleep anyway. I keep thinking of our Catherine with her first wee baby and me not there to help her," sighed Mary.

"She has Rose, love. Sure that woman is like a mother to everyone. Do you want to take money out of the savings and go over?" asked James.

Mary shook her head and said she would wait and see what Catherine's plans might be. In her last letter to them, she had spoken of traveling to Ireland when the baby was a little older.

"I can wait another while yet. What are you doing reading Thomas's letter in the middle of the night? Could you not sleep worrying about him?"

"He's a grown man and yet I still see him as a wee boy. Some of the tales he tells us makes my hair stand on end. Like the one about meeting the Indians. I'm fearful he may get pierced by one of their arrows if he's not careful," said James.

"They seemed by all accounts to be friendly towards him, but it worries me that he may come across more savage types. Still, this is what he has chosen to do, and we are blessed to have his wee Eliza with us in his absence," replied Mary.

"The Indians cannot be blamed for wanting to live in peace in their own land. We of all people should know what that feels like," said James. "Do you recall in his last letter what he said about those Choctaw people who sent money over for the starving of Ireland, and them with nothing themselves?"

"I do indeed, bless their kindness. How did you remember that name? I was telling Maggie about it and for the life of me I couldn't think what they were called," said Mary.

"Reading the words helps things stay in the head. Sure doesn't a kindness the likes of that, coming from strangers, deserve to be remembered?"

"I'm thankful I cannot read so, for there are some things best forgotten and our tragic past is one of them. I'm off back to bed. Come with me James. No good will come of fretting over things we cannot change."

"I know, love. I accepted that a long time ago and it has given me a measure of happiness that has evaded Michael Kiernan. Its men of his character that can bring about change, but it will break him doing so. I fear he is already a broken man."

CHAPTER THIRTY-ONE

Michael had been watching the comings and goings of Henry Armstrong for almost a month and had come up with a plan. He needed to meet him alone, in a place where there was no chance of them being disturbed. Ensuring there would not be an army of militia waiting to ambush him, was Michael's biggest problem. In spite of the fact that no warrant had been issued for his arrest, as soon as it was known that he was in the country, there would be an alert sent out. Michael's past experience convinced him he would be harassed and followed by the constabulary, while they waited for him to put a foot wrong. He hadn't gone to so much trouble keeping himself hidden, to risk being discovered because of a moment of carelessness.

Michael had learned of a certain married lady that Armstrong had become involved with, his visits to her a regular occurrence. They coincided with the departure of her husband on his frequent business trips to Dublin.

Michael was grateful for the food and shelter afforded him by an elderly widow, who needed help with her farm. She accepted his story of being on the run from the militia as a deserter, and he knew instinctively that he could trust her to be discreet.

The close proximity of Henry Armstrong's lodgings meant an easy trek across a few fields for Michael, enabling him to maintain a close watch on the district inspector's activity.

It didn't take him long to realize the businessman's journey to Dublin took place on the same day every fortnight.

On the occasion of the next illicit rendezvous, Michael took a bag containing his possessions from where it was hidden in an outhouse. The old stone building attached to the widow's cottage had been serving as his sleeping quarters. He emptied out the contents of the bag onto a bed of straw and checked each item meticulously. His pistol was loaded and he had enough ammunition to see him through the task that lay ahead. The last item he checked was a small bottle of chloroform wrapped inside a piece of cloth. He had stolen it from a midwife's house the week before.

The ass and cart he surreptitiously borrowed from the widow, made little noise on the grassy track as Michael drove it through the darkness. When he reached his destination, he brought the cart to a halt and jumped down, tying the reins to a fence, before disappearing into a nearby field.

As was his custom, to avoid suspicion, Henry Armstrong had instructed the cab driver to leave him at a tavern, around the corner from his destination. He went inside and ordered a whiskey, which he drank quickly, impatient to be in the company of his mistress. When he was sure the carriage was gone, the district inspector returned to the street and made his way along a row of middle class houses. The blow to his head came so suddenly, he never even heard the swish of the weapon as it sliced through the air.

Michael stepped out from the shadows to pick up the stricken man from the ground, quickly pouring a small bottle of whiskey over both of them as he did so. Making his way to the edge of the town, he exaggerated a stagger under the weight of his burden. Earlier that day, Michael had changed into his good suit, and to anyone who might see them, it would look as if he was helping a friend who had passed out from drink. The smell of alcohol would be convincing enough. Crossing over a bridge, Michael tossed Armstrong's pistol into the fast running water below.

It wasn't until he had put a good distance between himself and the lights of the town that Michael risked laying his victim on the ground. He looked around him, peering into the shadows. Once or twice along the way, he had the strongest feeling of being followed, but nobody had confronted him. Armstrong was a heavy man to start with but had put on even more pounds from his good living of late. In case he should recover too quickly from the blow to his head, Michael held a cloth soaked with chloroform over the district inspector's mouth and nose. There was a moment of resistance before Armstrong's body went limp once again.

Dragging the unconscious man through two fields was not an easy task, and Michael was thankful to hear the donkey's loud braying echo through the still air, as he drew close. He bound Armstrong's hands and feet securely and made sure he gagged him well, in the unlikely event of him coming round before reaching their destination.

"Well, it's done now. There's no going back, I'll finish what I've started," Michael whispered into the blackness surrounding him

CHAPTER THIRTY-TWO

There were very mixed emotions at Brigid Kiernan's reunion with her old friends. James and Mary had travelled on their cart to the quayside in Dundalk, to meet her as she stepped off the boat from Liverpool.

"You haven't changed a bit, Brigid. I would know you anywhere."

"Oh, Mary, I've aged ten years since I got the news about Francis. But you look as young as ever. This man of yours must be looking after you well. Treats you like a queen, does he?"

James had helped both women onto the cart and was handing Brigid her bag as she spoke.

"I keep telling her she should count her blessings, having a man the likes of me around the house, but do you think she listens? Not a bit of it," he replied in mock despair.

"You can take him back to America with you so, if you still hold him in such high regard by the end of the week. I usually have to hoist my skirts and haul myself up onto the cart without any assistance," Mary joined in with the friendly ribbing. "Don't let James's wee display of manners fool you, Brigid. He'll have you gutting fish and picking up his majesty's manure in no time."

After a good bout of laughter, Brigid asked Mary what she meant by 'his majesty's manure' and laughed again at her answer.

"Do you not think Rí is a foolish name for an ass? I cannot bring myself to say it, so I call him His Majesty," said Mary.

"You should hear her when she thinks nobody is about," said James. *"And how are you today, Your Majesty? Do you need a scratch behind your ear, or on your rump?* Ask the children, Brigid, they'll tell you it's true."

"Why James McGrother, I do believe you're jealous of an ass," teased Mary.

"And well I might be, sure I'm still waiting to have my rump scratched. I won't hold my breath."

Mary reached out and tickled her husband behind his ear, "Ahh, there you are now, you poor, neglected, unfortunate man."

Brigid joined in with her friends' laughter, breathing the sea air deep into her lungs. Old memories came flooding back and for the first time since receiving the news of her son's death, Brigid felt more like her old self. Thoughts of Michael forced their way into her head but instead of banishing them, as was her custom, she let them stay. As James and Mary continued in their friendly banter, Brigid looked around the landscape of her youth.

The gentle slopes of the Cooley Mountains as they reached out into the sea, gave the impression of a protective arm encircling the bay. Women and children gathering cockles from the rocks along the shore, waved at the cart as it passed by and it seemed to the visiting emigrant as if time had stood still in the village of her ancestors.

As the cart turned a corner in the road, her old family home came into view and Brigid's eyes filled with tears. When she noticed how quiet her companions had become, she dabbed her face with the end of her skirt and apologized for acting like a baby.

"Who lives there now?" Brigid asked.

"One of the Sharkeys. He fishes with Joseph Matthews. When his father died, Joseph kept the boat going and two of the Sharkey boys are still on his crew," said James.

"They're men now, married with children, like the rest of us. Joseph's eldest boy would have been nine this year but he died of –," Mary cut herself short.

"You don't have to be so mindful of your words around me," Brigid assured them, seeing her friend's discomfort. "Francis is gone and the sooner I accept it, the better. I know in my heart that once I have knelt at his grave I will begin to heal, for I haven't yet said goodbye to him."

The children knew there would be gifts from America and waited patiently until the meal was over. Mary's two eldest girls had prepared the food and beamed with pride as Brigid praised them for their culinary skills.

"So you are my namesake," she said to the young girl sitting by her side.

"I am. Ma always told me she named me after three different women and you are one of them."

"Well now, did she tell you who I'm named after?" asked Brigid.

"Saint Brigid of Faughart."

171

"That's very true, but it was also my grandmother's name and as I was the eldest girl, it was passed on to me."

"You can call me Breege, if you like, everyone else does," Mary's daughter smiled back.

"Why that's what we call my youngest girl. She was named after me. Now I have two fine young ladies as namesakes. You will have to come to America and meet her – when you are old enough to escape from your mother's clutches. A girl can make a fine life for herself there," Brigid smiled across the table at her old friend.

"Don't you go putting ideas of that sort into my daughter's head, Breege would never leave her old Ma. Would you, girl?" Mary was smiling outwardly but the mention of another of her children emigrating touched a nerve.

"Ah sure, I'd only go for a wee visit, Ma. I'll start saving my money as soon as I begin to earn a wage, Mrs. Kiernan," Breege turned to her mother, "Can I go out now to meet my friends, Ma?"

No sooner had Mary nodded her head, than the children jumped up from the table and headed for the door. Even Mary-Anne, carrying Eliza in her arms, raced outside. The two women laughed, knowing full well half the children in the village would be waiting to see what great treasures had been brought from America.

As soon as his offspring had left the cottage, James excused himself to make preparations for a night of fishing. When the neighbours saw the McGrother children and

172

their father leave the house it was a signal for them to pay their respects. After the usual condolences were offered to Brigid on the death of her son, a ritual of questions and answers took place. Mary made endless cups of tea while Brigid patiently satisfied the visitors' curiosity about life in a big American city. Any positive report she could give regarding a relative or neighbour brought great joy. Not wanting to disappoint anyone, she was soon making things up for those anxiously seeking good news of a loved one.

When the last visitor had left them alone, the two women tidied the parlour before setting out on a walk as the evening drew in.

"Would you like me to go with you to the graveyard in the morning, Brigid?"

"I would rather go there by myself, Mary, but I think I will leave it for a day or so. I'm not quite ready just yet."

"That's grand, Brigid. You'll know yourself when the time is right. It's a blessing that Michael is away on his travels in America, you don't need any more trouble on your shoulders," Mary linked her friend's arm.

"He's the last person I would want to see right now. The letter the children received just before I boarded the ship for Liverpool was sent from New Orleans and that's even further away from here than New York is."

"The further the better, Brigid. That's what I say."

The two women walked along in silence, happy to be in each other's company once again. Passing by the boats, they waved at the men tending nets and tackle, in preparation for a night of fishing.

"Do you miss Ireland at all? It doesn't sound like you do from the way you spoke of America to the children."

"Of course I do, Mary. I'm at times so homesick I cry myself to sleep. But my children are well settled now and I'm earning a good living from my lodging house. Did I tell you that the bank has agreed to lend me the money to purchase a second one?"

"Two houses? Why Brigid Kiernan, soon you'll be too high and mighty to talk to any of us," laughed Mary.

Later that evening, Maggie joined the family for a late meal. James was out in the bay on one of the boats and had high hopes of a good catch, the previous two nights fishing having brought in a bounty.

As he had been very quiet all through supper, Brigid turned her attention to Jamie.

"Well young man, you've been as silent as a church mouse. Do you not have any questions for me? Or have your sisters used them all up?"

"I have one question I'd like to know the answer to," Jamie replied.

"Go on then. Ask away," said Brigid.

The young boy looked from one of his sisters to the other. Breege was feeding Eliza small pieces of bread dipped in broth while Mary-Anne wiped a stream of dribble from the baby's chin.

"Have you ever seen a baby with no head, Mrs. Kiernan?" he asked.

Jamie's two sisters froze.

"What kind of a question is that, son?" Mary was shocked. "Babies in America are just the same as they are here. I'm sorry, Brigid. That's an awful thing to ask a person."

Jamie had anticipated the discomfort of his sisters, which was exactly why he brought up the subject, but his mother's reaction surprised him. Not sure if it was prudent to continue, he took another mouthful of bread.

"Don't mind me," laughed Brigid. "He can ask me anything he wants. No, Jamie, I can't say as I've ever laid eyes on a baby, or anyone for that matter, that didn't have their head on. The nearest thing that comes to mind is a headless chicken, but sure you must have seen one or two of those yourself."

Jamie was now perched on Brigid's knee. She was enjoying the innocence of the young boy and had drawn him onto her lap.

"Don't encourage him, Mrs. Kiernan. Ma should wash his mouth out with soap. Come on, you," Mary-Anne had grasped her brother's arm and was dragging him away from the table.

"Leave him be, girl. What's come over you all of a sudden? Those kind of morbid thoughts are always floating around a boy's head, but they are not usually so inclined to give voice to them," said Maggie, frowning at her nephew.

Poor Jamie was beginning to regret having asked such a controversial question. He had a distinct feeling it was going to backfire on him. As soon as his sister loosened her grip on him, he retreated to the safety of their visitor's lap.

"Come on, now, my wee man. Tell me, what prompted you to ask such a question," coaxed Brigid.

"I heard the girls talking about it one night when they thought I was asleep."

Mary-Anne and Breege were making their way to the door, when their mother's voice stopped them in their tracks.

"Get straight back here to the table you two. What have I said about frightening your wee brother with your ghost stories? See what you've done now?"

"Sorry Ma, why don't we talk about something else?" Mary-Anne returned to sit beside Brigid. "What is school like in America, Mrs. Kiernan?" she asked.

Maggie, who was never one to let the chance of a bit of entertainment slip by, insisted that Jamie explain himself more fully. The young boy avoided the glares of his sisters by looking from his mother to his aunt and finally to the woman whose knee he had taken refuge on.

"Is it true that a man has to do it lots of times to make sure the baby has a head?" asked Jamie.

After a few seconds of awkward silence had elapsed, pandemonium ensued. Mary-Anne was first out the door with Breege hot on her heels, having flung Eliza on top of her aunt's lap. Their mother chased after them, leaving Brigid and Maggie choking back the laughter.

"What does 'it' mean, Auntie Maggie?"

Jamie was more determined than ever to get an answer. If he was going to be thrashed by his mother and his sisters he had no intention of suffering in vain.

"I think you should ask your daddy that question," said Maggie with a glint in her eye. "A good time might be when he brings you with him to mend the nets. I'm sure one of the other fisherman could tell you, if your father doesn't know. They are a very wise breed of men. Would you not agree, Mrs. Kiernan?"

CHAPTER THIRTY-THREE

Deep into the woods, it became impossible to make any further progress with the cart, so Michael unhitched the donkey. Fortunately for him, the district inspector was still out cold, so it was just a matter of slinging him across the back of the animal for the rest of the journey.

When he reached his destination, Michael was worn out from pulling the reluctant donkey up a very steep incline. Inside a crudely made shelter he leaned back against a wall of cold stone, listening to Henry Armstrong slowly regain consciousness. It was so dark and quiet, the district inspector was convinced he was alone and began to struggle against his constraints.

Allowing his prisoner to expend his energy while listening unseen from the opposite side of the small, cave-like space, Michael smiled to himself, savouring every word shouted into the darkness.

"There's not a soul about for miles. You are wasting your breath."

"Who's there?" Armstrong was taken aback to discover he was not alone. "What do you want from me? If it's money, I have savings."

"I'm not interested in your money, but there *is* one thing I want from you, Armstrong, and I fully intend on taking it. However, you can answer a question, if you like. Why do you harbour such hatred for the Irish? If you do not wish to share your reasons, it's of no consequence to me. You are a dead man already," said Michael.

"If I tell you, of what benefit will it be to me?"

There was a few moments of silence, before the answer sliced through the blackness between them.

"Your death will be clean and swift. Otherwise, I will make sure that you suffer intolerable pain before the end," said Michael.

An owl hooted in the distance while the district inspector considered his options. Leaning against a rough stone surface, he became aware of a small piece of rock sticking into his back. Working his hands up towards his shoulder blades, Armstrong began rubbing the ties that bound his wrists against the jagged surface. To give himself the time needed to free his hands, he decided to satisfy his captor's curiosity.

"My father was a peace loving man, a carpenter, but he went to the assistance of a fellow worker, who had become involved in a brawl with a drunken Irishman. Soon more of your brave countrymen joined in the foray and my father, along with his friend, was beaten to death."

"I'm sure you have done likewise to some poor unfortunate men yourself," snapped Michael.

"It was the price my mother had to pay that causes my hatred," Armstrong ignored the remark.

"How so? Did she give your father an extravagant wake?" Michael's tone was caustic.

"Some time after my father's death, when I was six years old, my mother entered the workhouse with myself and my baby sister. She took a fever and was gone within a fortnight. I maintain she died of a broken heart. My sister followed her not long afterwards and I was left orphaned and alone among strangers. Before she passed away, my mother made me take an oath to hate every man woman and child of this cursed land."

"Are you saying that you blame me and my kin for what befell your father?" asked Michael.

"I do, for you are of a savage breed. Not one of you is civilized. Are you going to tell me who you are, now?" asked the district inspector.

"Who do you think I am?"

Armstrong continued to work the rope between his wrists as he spoke, "By the accent I would say you are a Louth man. Am I correct?"

"You might be. Continue," said Michael.

"Stop with your games, McGrother. I know full well it's you. I should have paid more heed to your movements. That was lax of me," spat out Armstrong.

A harsh laugh cut through the darkness.

"McGrother? What makes you say that? Is it James McGrother you take me for?" said Michael. "You could not be more wrong. The years that you have spent watching him have all been in vain, Armstrong, for I can assure you James is nothing more than a stonemason, who fishes when given half a chance. The only time he has ever taken a life is when he draws a net from the sea. I don't think he has even killed a rabbit. I daresay it's his wife who lops the heads off their chickens for the pot."

The district inspector was confused by what he heard. If the man concealed by the darkness was not James McGrother, then he hadn't a notion as to who it might be.

"You've gone very quiet, all of a sudden. Can't you guess who I am?" there was no response to the question.

"Does the name Francis Kiernan sound familiar?" the voice cracked with emotion.

'I am well and truly a dead man,' thought Armstrong. "Michael Kiernan? But you are supposed to be in America. I have proof of it."

"I may be uncivilized by your standards but obviously I'm much cleverer than you. I have been here all along, watching your every move. Your good lady friend will not report you missing, for fear that her husband will discover her infidelity. By the time anyone else notices your absence you'll be buried deep in the ground. I have already dug your grave, Armstrong."

The district inspector squinted at the dark shape just three feet away from him. He had assumed it was part of the rocky wall until his captor announced his presence. As he listened to the voice of Michael Kiernan, he prepared to launch himself in its direction. The rope, which had been securely twisted around his wrists, had fallen away.

On the other side of the large boulder that formed part of Michael's crude shelter, sat Constable Masterson. As he listened to their conversation he prepared himself for the sound of a gunshot, which would force him to take action. He had been assigned to make sure neither man came down from the mountain. It occurred to him that both men shared an equal amount of bitterness, allowing hatred to cloud their judgement. He understood why the Brotherhood could no longer protect a man who acted purely on emotion, blinded by rage.

When a shot finally rang out, Constable Masterson's body automatically jolted and he was on his feet immediately. There was so much thick cloud covering the moonless sky, not even a trace of light from a star shone through. After a moment of complete silence, with the rapid beating of his heart sounding in his ears, Masterson announced his presence, giving warning that he was armed. A man's voice from inside the crude shelter replied, stating that he too had a gun.

"District Inspector Armstrong, you're alive."

"Of course I am. Do you think I would allow one of his sort get the better of me? How did you find us, Masterson?"

The sound of a shot bounced off the stone walls and Armstrong slumped to the ground. When the young constable knelt by his victim's lifeless form, he was surprised to find his aim had been so accurate in such bad light. He found a pistol lying on the ground beside Armstrong and pushed it to one side. The place where he had seen Michael Kiernan dig a grave was only a few yards away, and it wasn't long before Henry Armstrong's body was buried deep in the stony clay. His final resting place was concealed by neatly cut sods of grass and scattered leaves.

Constable Masterson said a quick prayer over the grave before going back to where Michael Kiernan lay inside the shelter. He sat on the ground outside to rest awhile, leaning his back against a large wall of rock. Like his father, Masterson was English and of the Protestant faith, but his mother had been raised a Catholic by her Irish parents – a fact he had kept well hidden from Armstrong. As Masterson was saying one of his mother's prayers for Michael, a loud moan interrupted him.

Scrambling to where the sound had come from, he found Michael reaching out to a bag lying nearby.

"I thought you were dead," said Masterson picking up the dusty cloth bag.

"I need . . . chloroform . . . p-please," groaned Michael.

The constable took out a small bottle and placed a few drops onto a piece of fabric before handing it over. "Here, this will ease the pain. You're in a bad way."

"Who are you? Is Armstrong about?" asked Michael, having inhaled a little of the chloroform.

"He's dead, I killed him myself. I've been watching both of you for over a week now. Why couldn't you just leave well enough alone? He would have been taken care of in time."

"It wouldn't have been soon enough for me," replied Michael.

As the clouds dispersed, the full extent of Michael Kiernan's injuries were plain to see and Masterson knew he didn't have much time left.

"Can I do anything for you?" he asked.

"A little water, please. Over there," Michael pointed to an old chipped jug.

"I should tell you I'm a constable," said Masterson.

"Obviously one who sympathizes with the cause," smiled Michael. "I'm not going to last much longer, you don't have to stay. I won't be going anywhere except to meet my maker."

"I'll stay. Are you sure there's nothing more I can do for you?" Masterson again asked, noting that the injured man favoured his left hand in holding the jug and the cloth. "Would you like me to give someone a message?"

Michael took another whiff of chloroform as a sharp pain went through him. He could feel his life slipping away and a sudden fear took hold of him.

"I was never much of a writer as a child. Until I lived in America, I never appreciated the advantage of such a skill. It was my son, Francis, who taught me. When I learned that my wife was in Ireland I wrote her a letter telling her that I could no longer live with the remorse and grief of my son's death," Michael coughed, then waited to catch his breath. "It will be delivered tomorrow to the house of an old friend, where she is staying. He is also to receive a letter, with directions as to where my body can be found."

"You have planned it well, I'll give you that, Michael," said Masterson.

"Not well enough. I had hoped that Armstrong's whereabouts would never be discovered."

"Your secret is safe with me. After all, it was a bullet from my own weapon that killed him," the constable held out a hand.

Michael shook it, smiling weakly. He asked Masterson to pour the rest of the chloroform onto the cloth and hold it over his mouth until he passed out.

"I'm a coward at heart. I would rather go off in my sleep, given the choice."

"No, Michael," said the young constable as he poured out the contents of the bottle. "There isn't a cowardly bone in your body, may God have mercy on your soul."

In one swift movement, Masterson placed the cloth over Michael's nose and mouth, holding it down until long after his struggling came to an end. When he was sure there was no pulse, the constable put the pistol that Armstrong had dropped, into Michael's left hand and arranged his posture to that of someone who had shot himself.

Before leading the donkey down the mountain to where the cart had been left the night before, Constable Masterson removed all trace of Armstrong and himself. It was important that when the body was discovered it would be assumed that Michael Kiernan had taken his own life. *'I just gave you a little help on your way, my friend,'* Masterson said to himself.

CHAPTER THIRTY-FOUR

The young man standing cap in hand on James's doorstep, held out a small package along with a letter. He explained that his grandmother had given her word to the sender that it would be delivered to the McGrother house in Blackrock. James recognized the writing straight away and took a coin from his pocket.

"Take this for your trouble, son, and thank your grandmother for me."

"She wouldn't want me to take any payment. The man that gave it to her was a deserter from the militia and had been hiding out on her property, working for his keep. She fears he may be in trouble and in need of help," the young man explained. "I hope you find him, he's been missing since yesterday, along with my grandmother's ass and cart. This morning I found them but no trace of your friend."

"Well I'm much obliged to the both of ye. Will you have a bite to eat before you leave?" asked James.

Declining the offer, the young man bade farewell and walked towards a donkey that was grazing by the roadside.

"My grandmother will be anxious for me to bring back her cart, she has a pile of logs that your friend chopped, waiting to be delivered to some of her neighbours."

Once inside the cottage, James handed the letter to Brigid, while he unravelled the twine that bound the small parcel of newspaper. Inside was a note and the string of seashells that was so familiar to James. Michael had written instructions on where his body could be found and when he had finished reading, James looked up at Mary. The sadness on his face was enough to tell both women the news was not good.

"I never did learn to read, James. Would you, please?" Brigid held out her letter with a shaking hand.

"He's been here, in Ireland, all along," said James.

Tears were shed by all three as they listened to Michael's last words to his wife and children.

"He asks that we bury him with Francis," James looked up at Brigid.

"Of course he should be with his son. If I couldn't keep them apart in life, I'm not going to do so in death," the distraught woman replied.

"James, think carefully before you go rushing off. What if this is a trap?" asked Mary. "It's possible that Michael was forced to write such a note. He says in his letter that Armstrong will never again persecute us, but what if it is he that is waiting for you?"

James opened his hand and held out the seashells. "No, love, it's not a trap. Michael would never have sent these if it was. Matthew Clarke will come with me. Don't worry, Brigid, we'll bring him home."

It was two very sombre men who made their way to the next county to collect the body of Michael Kiernan. Until they saw it for themselves, neither man wanted to believe that he had taken his own life. James had a glimmer of hope that his friend may have changed his mind at the last minute.

"Michael might not have carried out his plan. What do you think, Matthew?" James blurted out after a long silence.

"Or he could be lying injured when we get there," his companion replied. "But we should prepare ourselves for the worst, James."

When they arrived at the foot of a small, wooded mountain, James unhitched the donkey and led him up a rough trail. Matthew looked around, making sure they had not been followed.

"How did you know about this place?" he asked.

"Michael's father brought the two of us here when we were younger, on one of my visits to Blackrock. His brother lived in that old ruin back there. After his wife and children died of famine fever, Michael's uncle took the boat to America. The landlord had his house tumbled as soon as he'd gone. There's a bit of a cave near the top, among the trees, that would afford some shelter. It's there we'll find Michael."

"There's only one Kiernan left in the parish now. It saddens me to think of so many families lost to us, James, with not a trace left behind, but a pile of old stones. No matter how desperate I was, I could never bring myself to leave."

"Myself and Maggie are the only ones in my family to remain here," said James. In spite of all the times I left Ireland, I still came back. Some of us are drawn home to our roots,

Matthew. It's a pull that's hard to resist, like rowing against the current."

"Aye, that's true enough, James. My own son had fully intended on returning but the longer he's away, the more settled he's become."

"The last time I was with our Thomas we spoke about the way things are for the likes of us, the fishermen, the labourers, the factory workers. He told me of great changes that are on the way."

"His generation will see it, James, God willing," said Matthew.

"Do you know what Thomas told me, while we sat in a boat looking across the bay? He said, *'There is a turning of the tide, Da,'* and I'm inclined to agree with him. He smiled as he said it, his face full of hope and dreams, but when I looked into his eyes I saw Michael Kiernan, and it chilled me to the bone. I pray he never ends up like this, with a friend on the way to collect his body."

James had stopped walking and was staring ahead at a group of large boulders. The look on his face was enough to tell Matthew they had reached their destination.

"I'll stay here with the ass and give you some time alone, James. I think we both know what you'll find there. Call out when you need me."

The branches and pieces of broken planks strewn across the boulders were signs that someone had made a shelter among the rocks. James hoped with all his heart that he would find it empty. Softly, barely above a whisper, he called out Michael's name. There was no response, even the birds seemed to hush their voices.

With a rush of panic, James bent down and dived into the space between the rocks. Michael was half sitting up, staring at him. The thought that he might still be alive flashed through James's head. As soon as he took hold of his friend's hand, the icy feel of it told him a different story. This was not the first time that James had discovered the body of a loved one, but it was just as painful as ever, in spite of the fact that he had been expecting it.

Sitting on the ground at Michael's side, James told him about Brigid's visit, speaking as if in conversation with him. He imagined he could hear his friend's voice and even his laughter. When he could no longer keep up the pretence, great sobs forced their way to his throat. It was too much for James, being in a place that reminded him of his childhood, alongside his old friend, with whom he had shared the best of those early years.

James cried for Michael and for his son Francis. He cried for his Uncle Pat and Aunt Annie and for his stillborn children that Mary had never stopped grieving over. He wept bitterly for his own parents, even though he couldn't remember them. Just when he felt drained of every tear in his body, he shed some more – for himself and the pain he was in. It was as if a hand of grief and despair had curled its fingers around his heart, piercing it through with long sharp nails. It squeezed so tight, James was sure he was about to meet his own end and die right where he was sitting, at Michael's side.

Finally, the pain eased and James went out to join Matthew. He was relieved to see that his companion was nowhere to be found and that he had not heard him weeping. Making his way to a stream that ran nearby, James found Matthew sitting on a rock, the donkey grazing beside him.

"I'm sorry I kept you waiting so long, I got a bit upset. He's gone, Matthew. Michael is gone. Will you help me carry him out?"

Matthew turned around, not surprised to see swollen red eyes on his friend's face. He had guessed the news was bad as soon as he heard James's cries coming from the shelter. It was then he had moved out of earshot and found the stream.

"I'm sorry, James, truly I am. Let's go bring him home."

CHAPTER THIRTY-FIVE

"How is she?" asked James.

"How do you think?" replied Mary. "It's as if poor Brigid has buried her husband and her son on the same day. I felt sure as soon as she saw the open grave it would be too much for her. She's a strong woman, I'll give her that. A lot stronger than when she was younger."

"Aye, you're not wrong there. Has she said whether or not she'll stay a wee bit longer?"

Mary sighed and looked at James, her eyes full of sadness, "She's not going back for another week. She wants to see the headstone put on the grave before she leaves. I fear this will be the last time we'll see Brigid in Ireland, by the way she's talking."

James pulled Mary onto his lap. They were alone in the parlour and he kissed her damp cheek, wet from tears that were beginning to flow.

"Let go of your grief, love, there's just the two of us here now. You've been holding it in for Brigid, haven't you?"

"I'm not grieving for Michael as much as for myself, James, and I feel bad about that. I don't want to say goodbye to Brigid, I feel in my gut this time it's for good."

Knowing only too well what his wife was talking about, James assured her there was nothing wrong in feeling sorry for herself. He knew from experience it was difficult to change what was in the heart. If that was an easy thing to do, then Michael would still be alive and James himself would be in America.

"You should have heard me wailing like a banshee up that mountain, when we found Michael. I'm thankful that Matthew Clarke had taken the ass off out of earshot, to quench its thirst. I cried for Ireland, Mary, and I'm not ashamed to tell you that."

James wrapped his arms around his wife and they sat there, Mary weeping into his shirt, until the light began to fade. There was something that James had wanted to say to Brigid but the opportunity never presented itself.

"Mary, you must tell Brigid never to breathe a word of what Michael said in his letter to me about Armstrong. I've been told he's missing and that means there will be hell to pay. As sure as you are sitting here with me, Michael had something to do with it. I pray that his secret has gone with him to the grave."

On the morning that she was to board a boat for Liverpool, Brigid paid one last visit to Haggardstown graveyard. As she placed some flowers from Mary's garden on the mound of freshly dug soil, she glanced across the headstones to where her friends stood.

James and Mary were arm in arm by the graveside of his aunt and uncle. Brigid could tell they were praying and felt bad that no thought of a prayer had entered her own mind. She sat on one of the large stones that James had carefully chosen to place around the grave.

"Michael, you take care of our son now. Do you hear me?" Brigid whispered, "I don't know why I'm even wasting my breath, sure you never listened to me when you were alive.

Francis is most likely the one looking after you now, keeping you from starting a riot in Heaven and getting yourself thrown out."

That thought brought a smile to Brigid's face and she gently patted the soil covering her two men. A vivid memory of Francis, laughing with his brothers and sisters, came to mind and something snapped in Brigid. Her light patting of the earth turned to a frantic pounding and she threw herself on top of the freshly cut flowers Mary had made into a posy that morning.

The sound of Brigid berating Michael and crying for her son brought her friends rushing across the graveyard. James had to lift her up, holding her tightly as she struggled to get out of his grasp.

"Let go of me. I want my son," Brigid's voice grew loud and shrill. "I need to hold him one more time. Francis. *Francis. FRAN*" –"

Mary slapped her friend across the face, taking James by surprise as much as Brigid.

"I'm sorry, love. Getting hysterical won't bring him back and will do you more harm than good," said Mary.

Brigid's soft whimpering was too much for James and he manoeuvred the broken hearted mother into Mary's arms.

"She can't travel alone in this state. Someone will have to go with her. This would be a good time for you to pay a visit to Catherine and see your new grandchild," said James.

"Come on, Brigid. We'll go back to the house. James is right in what he says. I was planning on taking a trip over to Catherine in a month or so, I'll just go a bit sooner. Sure we can have a grand time together on the journey to Liverpool and before you know it, you'll be back with your children in America. They must be sorely missing you, Brigid."

"Would you do that for me? Oh, Mary, it would mean so much to have you with me. I promise, I shall be fine once I'm on my way to New York, I have a powerful longing to embrace my children. Thank goodness the journey doesn't take as long as it used to."

As James helped a much calmer Brigid onto the cart, Mary climbed up on the other side, thankful that her friend had not waited to break down when she was alone on board the steamship to Liverpool.

"That's the spirit, Brigid. Your children will need their mother to be strong for them," said Mary, "If you feel up to it, we can take the boat together in the morning."

CHAPTER THIRTY-SIX

When Patrick Gallagher walked through the door of his one bedroomed, back to back, terraced cottage in Sunderland, he was almost knocked off his feet as his wife dived into his arms.

"Look at the state of you now. You're wearing half the quarry, love, with that dust all over yourself," Patrick held Catherine at arm's length. "Let me get out of these grimy clothes and then tell me what all the excitement is about."

"I'll have to tell you now or I'll burst. Ma is on her way over. She's probably in Liverpool by now. She got the boat across with her friend Brigid, you know, Michael Kiernan's wife, or his widow, I should say. As soon as –"

Michael Kiernan is dead?" her husband cut her short.

"Oh Patrick, I'm sorry to say it like that. I'm so excited about Ma coming to see us that I'm losing the run of myself."

"What happened to him? Was he sick? Did he have an accident?" Patrick lowered his voice. "Was he murdered?"

"Da sent a letter telling us about Ma's visit and when to expect her," Mary held the envelope in her hand. "He said Michael Kiernan shot himself by accident. Matthew Clarke and Da had arranged to meet up with him to go hunting and when they got there Michael was dead. Poor Da, finding his friend like that, it must have near broke his heart. They were like brothers, the two of them. Friends since childhood."

"That's a terrible blow for sure. It will do your Ma a power of good to spend some time with her grandson, it's a pity your Da couldn't have come with her," Patrick said this, in spite of being relieved he would not have to face his father-in-law too soon.

"I'll dish up your supper while you have a wash, love," Catherine said, placing a jar holding two red carnations in the centre of the table. "Look how well the flowers you bought me have kept, Patrick. They are almost a week old but fresh as ever."

Many miles away from the tiny house in Sunderland, across the Irish Sea, a sad and grieving man tended his friend's grave. James McGrother stooped to pick up a posy of dead flowers. It was the one that Brigid had placed there, before taking the boat back to Liverpool with Mary. He wondered what the two women were doing at that moment and hoped their hearts would not be as heavy as his own.

"Well now Michael, this is a sorry state of affairs isn't it? Me doing all the talking for a change and you not able to get a word in?" James ran his fingers along his friend's name, carved into the headstone.

"You knew I would see to it that you got a decent burial, alongside your son, didn't you, Michael? God forgive me for lying to a priest. If he had known you took your own life, he would never have allowed us to bury you in consecrated ground," James looked around to make sure no one could hear his whispers, "And I'll carry that secret to my own grave."

Before leaving the cemetery, James said a quick prayer in front of a small wooden cross.

It marked the final resting place of two people who had played a significant part in his life.

"If only I had you here to give me your sound advice, Uncle Pat. You always had a word of wisdom to offer me in times of trouble. I fear I'm not as well able to give my own family the same comfort," James sighed. "Still, all I can do is my best and hope it will suffice. Times are changing and Ireland is a very different place to the one I grew up in, and for the better, too. Our wee country will have a lot more to offer my grandchildren, by the time they have families of their own to rear. But I will have joined yourself and Annie by then, no doubt."

James left the graveyard and was deep in thought, as he coaxed Rí into pulling the cart along the road leading to the shore. Nearing the village he took note of the fine weather and calm water. A familiar contentment settled his troubled mind, as he realised his night would be spent on a boat out in the bay. James reminded himself that some things never seemed to change. In spite of famines, emigration and political upheaval, generations of Blackrock men had fished in those waters and kept their families housed and fed by doing so.

With the death of his friend so fresh in his memory, James pondered on his own demise and came to the conclusion, that he would like the sea to be his last resting place. Although it was a strangely comforting thought, he hoped it would not come about too soon. The turf had to be brought in for the winter and he had a new grandson to meet.

Besides, Mary would never forgive him if he left her without saying goodbye.

THE END

Book 4 will be published later in 2015.

References

Chapter Sixteen: *Grinders' Asthma*

Information on lung disease and the life expectancy for Grinders in the steelworks industry of the 1800's can be found at this link:
http://en.wikipedia.org/wiki/Sheffield_Outrages

Chapter Twenty-Four

In the mid-1800's there were multiple Fenian invasions into Canada in the hopes that British troops would be diverted from Ireland thus opening up an opportunity to gain a victory in the Irish struggle for independence. The following link will take you to some fascinating details on those events:
http://www.acsu.buffalo.edu/~dbertuca/155/FenianRaid.html

Chapter Thirty: *The Choctaw People's Generosity*

During the Great Irish Famine, the Choctaw nation of Oklahoma donated $170 in May of 1847 to the Irish Relief Committee, in New York. This was to a branch of the Society of Friends, known as Quakers. The remarkable thing about this generosity on the part of the Choctaw people, is that sixteen years earlier they were forced to leave their ancestral lands in Mississippi.

They were the first of the south eastern Native Americans to be relocated to a reservation in Oklahoma on what came to be known as "The Trail of Tears." On that sad journey, they lost almost half their people, unused to the colder climate and with insufficient nourishment for such a long trek.

It was President Andrew Jackson who pushed the Indian Removal Act through Congress in 1830, the Government subsequently spending the next thirty years forcing tribes to move westward, beyond the Mississippi River. The Choctaw people felt an affinity with the suffering of the Irish, who were being evicted and often forced to emigrate, due to famine and poverty.

The irony is, that Andrew Jackson's ancestral home was in Ireland, in County Antrim. His parents were Ulster-Scots, who settled in South Carolina in 1765, yet the Choctaw people were moved to help the Irish in their time of need, in spite of the suffering that one of Ireland's 'sons' had caused them.

Gary Whitedeer of the Choctaw is an internationally known artist, tribal chanter and dance leader. He has represented the Irish-Choctaw link on many occasions. In 2008 he presented the second Choctaw donation to Ireland when he gave it to the community resisting Shell's activities in Erris, County Mayo.

http://marsocial.com/2013/08/irish-choctaw-famine-link/

Author Bio

Jean Reinhardt was born in Louth, grew up in Dublin and lived in Alicante, Spain for almost eight years. With five children and three grandchildren, life is never dull. She now lives in Ireland and loves to read, write, listen to music and spend time with family and friends. When Jean isn't writing she likes to take long walks through the woods and on the beach.

Jean writes poetry, short stories and novels. Her favourite genres are Young Adult and Historical Fiction.

Follow her on:
www.twitter.com/JeanReinhardt1

Like her on:
www.facebook.com/JeanReinhardtWriter

Join her on:
www.jeanreinhardt.wordpress.com

Other books by the author:
A Pocket Full of Shells (Book 1 An Irish Family Saga)
A Year of Broken Promises (Book 2 An Irish Family Saga)

The Finding Trilogy: a young adult medical thriller.
   Book 1: Finding Kaden
   Book 2: Finding Megan
   Book 3: Finding Henry Brubaker

All books are in digital and paperback format on Amazon and Smashwords. They can also be ordered from The Book Depository and Createspace.

Acknowledgements

As always I'm extremely grateful to my Beta Readers for taking on the early drafts and giving me their honest feedback; Brenda, Pascaline, Ellen, Eileen, Carol and Elaine.

Thank you, Lukas, for posing for the front cover image.

Many thanks to Noel Sharkey (historian and poet)

The following books proved to be a great source of information in the writing of this story. They are full of well documented events and photographs of people whose families have lived in Blackrock for many generations, including my own:

The Parish of Haggardstown & Blackrock – A History by Noel Sharkey.
First Printed in 2003 by Dundalgan Press (W. Tempest) Ltd., Dundalk.

The Parish of Haggardstown & Blackrock – A Pictorial Record
Compiled and written by Noel Sharkey with photos by Owen Byrne.
Printed in 2008 by Dundalgan Press (W. Tempest) Ltd., Dundalk.

Made in the USA
San Bernardino, CA
27 December 2015